"What are you doing?"

The towel was barely larger than a hand towel and hardly covered CoCo, but she didn't care.

"Why aren't you dressed?" Rian asked, sitting up straight as an arrow, his eyes wide.

"I'm going out tonight. If you want to babysit me, fine, then you're going to have do it while I'm having some fun."

"Like hell you are. Now get some clothes on," he growled, and she taunted him with a smile.

"What? You don't like me in my towel? Is there something wrong?" she asked coyly, enjoying the sudden flush in his cheeks as she toyed with him. "I wonder what would happen if I did...this?" Then in a deliberate move she dropped the towel to the floor, and she could see Rian trying to swallow.

That's right, Rian Dalton...two can play games, but only one is going to win.

Me.

Dear Reader,

I love writing stories with characters who have a lot of growing to do. CoCo and Rian were two people who just needed that little push to become the best versions of themselves. And sometimes the best way to create change is to apply a whole lotta heat!

I had fun playing with these two characters and putting them in all sorts of trouble for the sake of a happily-ever-after, and I hope you do, too. This was my first two-book series with Blaze and I think I've found a fun new place to hang out. If you missed my first Blaze novel, *The Hottest Ticket in Town*, featuring Kane Dalton, you might want to check that one out, too!

Hearing from readers is a special joy. You can email me at alexandria2772@hotmail.com, or find me at kimberlyvanmeter.com or facebook.com/kim. vanmeter.37. Or mail me at PO Box 2210, Oakdale, CA 95361.

Happy reading!

Kimberly

Kimberly Van Meter

Sex, Lies and Designer Shoes

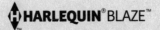

ISBN-13: 978-0-373-79861-2

Sex, Lies and Designer Shoes

Printed in U.S.A.

www.Harlequin.com

Kimberly Van Meter wrote her first book at sixteen and finally achieved publication in December 2006. She writes for the Harlequin Superromance, Blaze and Romantic Suspense lines. She and her husband of seventeen years have three children, three cats and always a houseful of friends, family and fun.

To all the people still living under the umbrella of others' expectations...step out. Don't be afraid to be who you are. An original is always worth more than a copy.

_**1**_

RIAN DALTON, CO-OWNER of Elite Protection Services, stared at the offer on the table and couldn't believe he was about to say this but the fact was, it wasn't enough to put up with CoCo Abelli. The hot-blooded heiress was a common enough sight in all the trendy Los Angeles clubs and the paparazzi loved catching her falling on her ass, slipping a nip or otherwise acting like the wild child she was.

And Rian was smart enough to steer clear of that hot mess. He regarded the older man awaiting his answer and said without regret, "Sorry, I can't take your money. You need someone who can do the job without bias and frankly, I know enough about CoCo to know that I don't want that headache—no matter how much money is put on the table. I can recommend a few highly qualified alternatives if you'd like…"

"I don't want second best for my daughter," Enzo Abelli, a paunchy man in a finely tailored suit, said in a thick Italian accent, his jowls jiggling as he shook his head. "You are the best. So I hire you. No exceptions."

"I'm flattered but I'm respectfully declining. The

fact is, CoCo is the worst sort of client—determined to do the exact opposite of what I tell her to do for her own safety—it's a headache I don't need." Rian was usually the charmer, the schmoozer of the two Dalton brothers, but he was taking a page from Kane's playbook by going with the blunt approach. He fished out his phone, prepared to give the man some digits, but Enzo wasn't finished.

"She is my only child. Perhaps I have indulged her too much. She is willful, spoiled to a fault, but that is not her fault. She has a good heart. Someone is trying to use my love for her against me. They are threatening to kill her if I do not give in to their demands. Without CoCo, everything I've worked for means nothing. I would pay any sum you desire if you would agree to take my case."

Rian wanted to shut the man down again but there was something about the sincerity in the older man's voice that tugged at his sense of right and wrong. The man—a billionaire three times over—was simply a father trying to protect his daughter. Rian didn't know what it was like to have a father who gave a damn about his kids—his own father had been a miserable son of a bitch who'd nearly killed him on several occasions. Hell, if it hadn't been for Kane, he'd probably be dead. So, hearing the desperation in Enzo's voice did something to a long-buried childhood wish that his father had been decent.

Sensing Rian was backsliding, Enzo pushed a little harder. "The FBI are working to find this miscreant and it should only take a few days, a week at the most, to end this nightmare. Surely you can take on a week? I would happily make it worth your while."

A week with CoCo? That was a tall order. Enzo would have to throw in a yacht.

It wasn't only that she was a handful and would likely make him want to punch a wall a few times, but CoCo was a drop-dead gorgeous blonde with a body that always turned heads—including his own.

He'd been at the same clubs, winding down, when he'd seen her the first time, all legs and hips, looking like a traffic violation in her tight dress and stiletto heels, and for a split second, he'd entertained the idea of introducing himself. But then he'd recognized her from the tabloids and he'd steered clear. The last thing the business needed was bad press from hanging out with the wrong people. That included CoCo and her little posse.

Just politely let the old guy down and chalk this one up to an unfortunate conflict of interest, the voice of reason told him but damn, if his mouth didn't start moving with its own agenda. "A week at the most?" Rian repeated and Enzo nodded vigorously. "All right. I can commit to a week. Anything after that, we'll have to find something else."

"Of course, of course," Enzo said, agreeing quickly. "Thank you, Mr. Dalton."

"Well, don't thank me yet. You haven't heard my terms. I hate to be the bearer of bad news but your daughter isn't known for following rules. And she's not going to like the rules I put down for her safety. It's your job to ensure that she listens, otherwise you're throwing good money after bad."

"She's stubborn but I will impress upon her the gravity of the situation," Enzo assured Rian. "She's young and impetuous but she's very bright. She will understand that this is necessary for her protection."

Will she? Parents were usually blind to their kids' shortcomings. If Enzo had half an idea of the shit his daughter was into, he'd probably have a heart attack. But that wasn't Rian's burden. He rose and shook Enzo's hand. The man, though nearing seventy-five, was robust and healthy, which probably explained why he was always seen squiring about women younger than his daughter. Money and fame—the greatest aphrodisiacs on the planet. "I'll do my best to keep Miss Abelli safe," he told Enzo. "By any means possible."

"You're a good man," Enzo said, pumping Rian's hand vigorously. "A good man, indeed. I will have the money wired to your account if you'll just provide the details to my manager."

Rian nodded and let himself out of the West Coast mansion owned by the Abelli family and wondered if he'd just sold his soul to the devil for a metric ton of cash.

Well, one way to find out.

"I LOVE LA," CoCo Abelli murmured as she stood out on the balcony of her mother's Malibu mansion, enjoying the oceanfront view of the palatial home. "Even the smog is glorious."

"You're cracked in the head," quipped her friend Stella Richards as she lounged on the bed, idly thumbing through a magazine. "Breathe that stuff long enough and your lungs will stop working. I should know—I think I have a permanent prescription for my inhaler."

CoCo ignored Stella and returned inside, already bored. She'd been in town for all of a week and everything thus far had been deadly dull. If she'd wanted peace and quiet, she would've stayed in Italy. "My mother is gone for a few months. Let's throw a party."

Stella perked up as CoCo knew she would. "Go on. I'm listening."

"I'm thinking, hire a DJ, get a mixologist, a little security to watch the gate…"

"God, yes, we don't need any crashers. Remember that last party when that loser production assistant made his way in? Kept pestering everyone to look at his script. As if anyone comes to a CoCo Abelli party to read." Stella rolled her eyes and climbed from the bed to walk into Azalea's huge walk-in closet. "Your mother has impeccable taste," she said with envy, grabbing a pair of heels. "Giuseppe Zanotti, Limited Edition, I could die. It's not fair that your mother gets first dibs on designer shoes just because your dad is a famous shoemaker. Honestly, they're not even married anymore. That's quite a perk."

CoCo shrugged. "Azalea knows how to negotiate." She snapped her fingers to get Stella's attention. "Back to the important stuff—the party. Should we go with a theme? Something fun?"

"I don't know, themes are so overrated unless it's Halloween or Christmas, you know?" Stella said, already bored as she replaced the shoes and exited the closet. "Did your mom leave her jewelry behind?"

"Not the good stuff."

"Figures. Although that rock she's sporting now… does it give her finger a cramp from wearing it all day? It's almost ridiculous."

CoCo didn't want to talk about her mother. Their relationship was strained on most days and now that she was married to a man CoCo found tedious and overbearing at the same time, they really had nothing productive to say to one another.

Although born in Milan, CoCo split her time between Europe and California—specifically, Los Angeles. And she really did love LA. Everything was wild and unbridled here, wealth was celebrated and she always found a good time running around the clubs, hanging out with movie stars.

It wasn't that Italy didn't have wealth—some of the wealthiest people in the world called Milan home—but it wasn't flaunted with opulent awareness as it was in the City of Angels. The obscenity of riches fascinated CoCo, as did the knowledge that in Los Angeles, bad girls got noticed and sometimes rewarded for their bad behavior, rather than chastised and hidden away for a month until they promised to behave themselves. European countries were far more reserved, it seemed, when it came to breaking rules, and CoCo found that boring.

Thankfully, when her mother divorced Enzo, Azalea had been crafty enough to wrangle a monstrous settlement out of her older ex-husband and thus CoCo had always split her time between continents without any discernible change in lifestyle.

And since her mother was often out of the country—such as right now—that meant CoCo had the run of her mother's Malibu mansion.

And there was no better place to have a raging party than a huge house with private beach access.

"Let's invite Guillermo to DJ," Stella suggested until CoCo made a face. "Oh, c'mon, just because you two hooked up and he blabbed about it doesn't mean he can't spin a mean set and you know it. Besides, he's the best and he always comes with Molly."

Molly, the street nickname for ecstasy, was always invited to a raging Hollywood-style party. The twenty-something crowd just didn't party without it. And it would be convenient if she knew exactly who was giving it out. Sort of like crowd control.

"I suppose that is a point in his favor," CoCo agreed, slowly warming to the suggestion. "But do not let me sleep with him. He may be good in the sack but he's as bad as a girl name-dropping to get into a club. He's got the loosest lips I've ever seen. And frankly, hooking up with him had been out of circumstance, not an extreme attraction, you know?"

"I get it. Slim pickings that night. Do you remember who I went home with that night?" Stella shuddered. "Rafe Dirk—otherwise known as The Dick—and not because he's well-endowed. Much to my extreme displeasure. He didn't even pay for my cab afterward!"

"What a dick." CoCo laughed. "Okay, pinkie promise that we go home with only those who have been previously approved. Do you have a target?"

Stella turned sly at the prospect of sharing. "You first."

"Chicken." CoCo bounced onto the bed with a grin. "Fine. I'm actually thinking of hooking up with Charlie Rogers… He's pretty cute and he's a great dancer, which means he knows how to move, if you know what I mean."

Stella gasped in total shock. "Are you kidding me? I hate to burst your bubble but he's totally gay. Sorry, babe."

"Are you sure?" CoCo asked. Stella nodded. "Well, that sucks," she said, sharply disappointed.

She sighed and flounced back on the bed, her plan totally derailed until Stella said, "Don't worry, I have someone you might like. Let's just focus on the party and then we'll worry about who we're shagging later. Those things should really happen organically, right?"

"I guess," CoCo grumbled as she rose on her elbows, frowning. "Wait a minute...you never said who you were targeting."

Stella grinned with a wink. "I know. It's a secret. Now, c'mon, let's get the party going. We have social media to post, a caterer to hire, a mixologist to find and a ton of other details to coordinate in eight short hours."

CoCo, happy to have something to look forward to, allowed Stella to drag her from the room. And just like that...everything was looking up.

2

AFTER FLASHING HIS CREDENTIALS, Rian drove through the gates of the Malibu mansion and gave his keys to the valet, shaking his head at the opulence of having a valet at a private party, but hey, this was LA and that was the norm. Having grown up dirt poor, sometimes the habits of the insanely wealthy baffled him. It was like landing on an alien planet and finding out all the inhabitants talked out of their butts. Well, that actually happened a lot in Hollywood, he thought with a private chuckle.

Music throbbed with an electric beat that vibrated his bones and he wondered how many complaints CoCo racked up with one of her parties. She was definitely violating the noise ordinance with that crap assaulting his ears. He wound his way through the teeming masses and ignored the drunken solicitations from the myriad of messed-up girls and made his way outside, looking for CoCo. He found her easily, the center of attention, with a group of stylish, nearly naked people dancing to the music from the DJ, who was moving to his own beat as he mixed music. Rian recognized the

DJ, Guillermo—otherwise known as The Dealer in certain circles—and wondered how the guy didn't have a rap sheet a mile long for all the shit he was into. He had a feeling that CoCo wasn't going to go quietly into his protection and he didn't want to draw unnecessary attention to himself so he decided the best way to handle the situation would be to get her alone.

And there was one way that usually worked.

Rian made his way to CoCo, wearing his confidence like an expensive suit. Women like CoCo responded to that alpha vibe even if they tried to pretend otherwise, at least that's what experience told him so that's what he was going with.

Walking straight up to her, ignoring the curious stares and the murmurs, he snagged CoCo's attention with a mesmerizing look that never failed to catch the ladies. Kane liked to call it Rian's "C'mere, girl" look and never missed an opportunity to razz him about it, but so far it'd served him well, and who was he to argue with success?

If Rian were a different kind of man and CoCo wasn't part of the job, he might be all over that sizzling Italian number. She was enough to make a man change his religion but Rian knew that beyond that model face and body was a headache and a half, and he didn't deal in drama.

CoCo's almond-shaped eyes narrowed with interest as she boldly appraised his body, the corners of her lush mouth tilting in an intrigued smile as he went straight to her. "Some party," he said by way of hello.

"And you are?" she asked, lifting one perfectly groomed eyebrow.

He leaned in, catching a whiff of her delicate perfume, and answered, "The man you're going home with," and her amused laughter tickled his insides.

"It's my house, so I'm not going home with anyone," she said, moving away with a sly grin that bordered on flirtatious, glancing over her shoulder as she added, "But maybe if you're lucky, you can stay, country boy."

And then she was gone, melting into the crowd, leaving him and his girl-gettin' smile behind. Well, hot damn. That hadn't worked as well as he'd hoped. Time for plan B, though admittedly, plan B…was a lot less fun.

He was also willing to bet CoCo wouldn't like plan B at all.

As FAR AS hosting parties went, CoCo held the distinction for holding the best, and this one was no exception, but for some reason she was bored out of her mind and wished everyone would just go home already. However, that wasn't likely to happen. It was only midnight and it was just getting rowdier. She surveyed the writhing masses grinding to the beat and she wondered if there was anything left to excite her. Poor rich-girl problems. She wanted to get away from the noise, and considered leaving altogether, but then she didn't trust all these people in her mother's home without some sort of supervision and opted instead to retreat to a less crowded area of the house.

As she pushed past the people clogging the entryways, she thought of the stranger who'd managed to gain entrance into the party. It was possible he was a friend of someone she'd invited but his was a face she wouldn't have forgotten.

It wasn't often that a guy managed to catch CoCo's

attention like that and it'd taken every ounce of self-control she had not to take the bait. Talk about a killer smile, and those eyes! He was the hottest thing she'd seen in LA thus far and that was saying a lot. CoCo ran in elite circles where handsome and rich were the norm.

But there'd been something rugged about the man, even though he wore a tailored suit and flashed a designer watch. Her father had always told her that you could tell a lot about a man by his watch and his shoes. Considering her father was a world-renowned Italian shoe designer, she took his word to heart. She wound her way past the throng of people, making her way to the kitchen to grab a bottled water and to escape the craziness for just a minute.

"CoCo, baby, there you are, I've been looking for that sweet ass of yours all night."

CoCo turned in time for Drake Pennington to drape himself over her as if she were his own personal coat-rack, and she rolled her eyes in irritation at the man's drunken pawing. *Sleep with a man once and he thinks he has the right to a booty call anytime he's horny.* She removed Drake's arm with a scowl. "Go somewhere and sober up," she said, trying to extricate herself from his grip as he pulled her to him. "It was a onetime thing and not likely to be offered again," she told him with distaste.

"Don't be like that, CoCo," he chastised her as he tried to nuzzle her neck, abrading her tender skin with his chin stubble. "You and I are like two mirroring souls, destiny and all that. It's a shame to let all that hot tail go to waste, baby. I got what you need right here."

"Poetic and total shit. You're drunk. Let me go," she

said. "Don't make me toss you out. I'm in no mood for your crap tonight."

Drake ignored her threat and squeezed her ass, eliciting a squeak of alarm as he pressed her against the stainless-steel refrigerator. "Here's how I see this going down… You and I are going to go to your room for a little privacy and we're going to relive some good times. Sound like a plan?"

"Sounds like a nightmare. You're a selfish lover and you slobber like a dog," she said coolly, trying to remain calm even though Drake was freaking her out. Maybe she'd underestimated Drake's feelings for her. Wouldn't be the first time a man fell in love with her after sex.

She pushed at him but he stuck like glue, the alcohol dulling his good sense. "You're embarrassing yourself," she said, mildly alarmed that Drake seemed deaf to her blatant answer of *hell no*. "Drake, stop it." But he continued to nuzzle her neck and slobber all over her as if she were an ice cream cone, which only brought back the unfortunate memory of sleeping with him. What had she been thinking? If she could go back in time… She shoved at him again, trying to put some space between them. "What are you doing, you idiot! I swear I'll scream and bring this whole party rushing in if you don't stop."

"Now you're talking. Let's do it in front of everyone. Kinky!"

Ugh! What a pervert! Was she going to have to scream to get him off her? Why'd she let Stella invite him? CoCo kicked up her struggle but just as she opened her mouth to yell for help, Drake was suddenly ripped away from her and tossed to the floor like a rag doll, and CoCo found herself staring at the hot stranger she'd talked to earlier.

"You really should pick better friends," he said, picking Drake up from the floor and manhandling him straight to the door before tossing him out. "Let him sleep it off on the front lawn."

Oh, thank God. That could've been embarrassing. CoCo's relief was short-lived as she realized he'd just vaguely insulted her. "Excuse me?" she bristled. "Do I even know you? How'd you get into my party?"

"You have a funny way of showing gratitude," he said. "A simple thank-you would be just fine."

"I don't recall asking for your help. I can handle Drake on my own. He's basically harmless."

"Yeah, it looked like you were doing a bang-up job of handling things. Tell me, at what point were you going to admit that you were in over your head? About the point when he started ripping your clothes off?"

"Don't be such an alarmist. That wouldn't have happened. Drake isn't a rapey kind of guy."

"Could've fooled me. In my world, when a woman says no, it means exactly that. Didn't seem that your friend was getting the message."

Her cheeks burned at the mere possibility that Drake might've taken things too far. Drake was pretty drunk. He probably wouldn't even remember getting tossed outside.

"Still choking on that thank-you?"

Smart-ass. "If I had something to be thankful for, I wouldn't have a problem saying it. But as I said, I had things under control," she maintained stubbornly, even if there was a niggling doubt that maybe Drake might've been a little too jacked up to listen to reason. "However, since *you* seem stuck on the need to hear it...thanks for handling a mildly embarrassing situation," she said stiffly. "Now answer my question... Just who are you?"

He sighed as if she'd just responded exactly as expected and found it disappointing, then said, "Glad you asked." He produced credentials and a business card, which she accepted with open confusion. *Elite Protection Services, Rian Dalton.* She regarded him with a faint frown as he continued. "Your father has hired me to watch over you for the next couple of days while the FBI figures out who's been threatening him."

She returned the card with an irritated exhale. "Chill out on the panic button. Your services aren't required. I don't need a babysitter. My father is just being overly protective."

"Your father started receiving death threats about a week ago. In the interest of your safety, your father has hired me to make sure that no one gets any bright ideas about kidnapping his only heir for ransom."

"As if that would happen," CoCo said, bored. "People don't get kidnapped. That happens on television and in the movies but not in real life."

"And here I thought you were smarter than that but apparently, you're pretty comfortable with the blonde stereotype."

She stared. Okay, that was definitely an insult. *What a jerk.* When her father had told her about the threats, she'd tried to reassure him that it was nothing but he'd been so freaked out. Now it seemed she should've worked harder to talk some sense into him. But first, she needed to send this prick packing. "As I said, your services aren't required. Thank you for your assistance earlier but I think we're done here."

"I don't work for you, sassy pants. I work for your father."

"Well, I'll call my father tomorrow and let him know that I can take care of myself."

"Fine by me, but until then, I'm your shadow."

She narrowed her gaze. "And just what does that mean?"

"Exactly what you think it means."

CoCo shook her head. There was no way she was going to be trailed by this man for the next few days. He was already stomping on her nerves. "That's not going to happen. I refuse. What then?"

"Then the next few days will be awkward and uncomfortable for us both. The fact is, your daddy paid me a shit-ton of money to watch over your spoiled ass and, pardon me, frankly I'm not sure you're worth the money, but it's his dime so here I stay."

"How dare you!" She'd never been so boldly dissed in her life and she didn't like it. "You don't have the right to talk to me like that."

Rian smirked. "Yeah, I call 'em as I see 'em and that's a fact. I know all about you, CoCo Abelli. For that matter, who doesn't? You're a spoiled heiress with daddy issues and you're always in the spotlight for doing something dumb. Usually getting drunk and falling all over yourself or something like that. Made quite a reputation for yourself and, to be honest, I didn't want this job. In fact, I tried to refuse, but your daddy seems to think that his daughter deserves the best so here I am. Far be it from me to refuse good money even if I think it's a fool's errand. So do us both a favor and march your butt into your room and stay there for the rest of the night, because this party is a security nightmare. You don't really think all these people are your friends, right?"

CoCo could only stare. No one spoke to her like that. No one! And it hurt. She was more than just a paparazzi payday. "Are you finished?" she asked. When Rian simply folded his arms across his chest and waited, she stared him down with all the European disdain she had flowing through her veins and said, "Not only are you finished with this job... I'm going to see to it that you never work in this town again."

"Good luck, honey. Better people than you have tried—and failed. But don't do me no favors. Being let go from this detail would be the biggest blessing of the year."

What could she say to that? He wasn't pulling any punches and she had no doubt that he was being truthful. He truly didn't want the job, which only made her feel like a boil on someone's butt. She wasn't going to win any arguments with him at the moment and she wasn't going to waste her time trying, especially when she was a bit dulled from all the alcohol. "I won't lower myself to your level, Mr. Dalton," she said icily. "Stay if you choose but I am not going to my room like some child. I have people to entertain."

"Ah, yes, the nip-slip hasn't quite occurred yet, right? Don't want to miss out on that."

She glared. "Screw you."

"No, thanks. I don't mix business with pleasure."

Her blood boiled but she wasn't about to make a scene. Lifting her chin, she turned on her heel and deliberately left him behind. She had to get away from that man. What was her father thinking hiring a thug like him?

She went straight to the bar and ordered a whiskey sour. She'd just managed to down it when Stella sidled up to her, nearly falling down drunk. "Who was that hottie you were talking to in the kitchen?" she slurred. "He's the freshest meat in this place. I call dibs!"

"You can have him," CoCo muttered even though she knew Stella wouldn't remember a thing they were saying. She was nearly at puke level.

"Have you seen Drake? He was looking for you. You two are so cute together…"

"Drake is a slime," she said, her thoughts still centered on Rian and how she'd like to wipe that smirk off his smug face. Stella giggled and CoCo wished her friend were at least halfway sober so she could tell her what'd happened, but she knew it was pointless to try to get Stella to focus right now. "Are you staying here tonight?" she asked.

"Only if I don't get lucky," Stella answered with a drunken giggle, swiveling around to survey the crowd with bleary eyes. "Now, where did Mr. Hottie run off to?"

She ought to sic Stella on Rian. That ought to keep him busy for a bit. But even as the uncharitable thought raced through her mind, she discarded it. The last thing she needed was Stella hooking up with the man her father had hired to protect her. It was bad enough he was here at all, no sense in making things worse.

Besides, if CoCo wasn't getting lucky—neither was her jerk of a bodyguard.

3

HE PROBABLY SHOULDN'T have come down so hard on her—she was the client's daughter after all. If Kane were here, he'd knock him in the head for running his mouth when he ought to keep it shut, but there was something about the woman that unhinged his jaw.

He wasn't a stranger to spoiled heiresses but CoCo Abelli took the ever-loving cake. The girl wouldn't know how to be grateful if someone had saved her life, which is exactly what her father was trying to do. Personally, Rian thought Enzo ought to cut his losses with this one, because she was clearly ruined beyond repair. The only thing CoCo cared about was herself or the next party. Maybe it would do her some good to have a little scare. But that wasn't his place. Maybe with some luck CoCo would convince her father that his services weren't needed and he could go on with his life. One could hope.

Throughout the night he kept an eye on CoCo as she partied until the wee hours of the morning, as if purposefully thumbing her nose at him, and by the time the sun rose and everyone had left Rian felt as wrung out as he had during a night watch in Afghanistan. Watching over this girl would be no picnic.

CoCo, her eyes red from a night of hard alcohol and who knew what else, ignored Rian and stumbled to her bed. He rounded up the rest of the stragglers and booted them from the house, finally able to breathe a little easier. The Malibu beach house wasn't the most secure location. Too many points of entry to defend. If someone were looking to kidnap CoCo, they could practically waltz in and snatch her without breaking a sweat. So that meant they weren't staying here for the next few days. He figured that news was going to go over like a turd in a punch bowl. He kind of relished the idea of giving her that news. He got the impression not many people told CoCo what to do and when. That was her problem. She'd been indulged way too much in her life. Time for a reality check. The fact that she didn't believe she was in any danger went to show just how naive she was.

He did another perimeter check and secured all the doors and then decided to take a catnap. He was a light sleeper by nature but his years in combat had trained him to sleep with one eye open. If anyone tried to get past him, he would know it.

He rarely dreamed or if he did he didn't remember the details. Sometimes when he woke he was left with a hazy idea that he'd dreamed of something but most times it was just a blank canvas. So why did he have the most vivid dream of CoCo? Sun-bronzed skin, a tiny bikini and that achingly beautiful body—correction, it wasn't a dream, it was a nightmare. He didn't want to be dreaming of CoCo like that. He didn't want to think of her in any way except as an annoying client. It was bad business to mess around with the clients.

After about two hours Rian's cell phone jerked him awake and he saw that it was Kane.

"Yeah, what's up?" he asked, rubbing the sleep from his eyes.

"I wanted to check and see how things are going with our newest client. I figured you were on the job last night. Everything cool?"

"I guess you could say that. She's a nightmare just as I expected. I chased off some guy mauling her in the kitchen and did I get an ounce of thanks? No. She's an ungrateful bitch and frankly, I'm thinking that giant payday wasn't nearly enough. Maybe I can tack on a handling fee for my pain and suffering."

"I thought you said that you tried to refuse the job."

"I did. I'm just cranky from getting two hours of sleep."

"You always were grouchy if you didn't get your full eight hours. You're such a prima donna. Do you have a plan for the next couple of days?"

"Try not to kill the woman myself?"

"Come on now, I'm serious. The Abelli account is a pretty big payday. Just treat it like any other."

Rian didn't need his big brother lecturing him. "This isn't my first rodeo. I know what I'm doing. If I need your help, I'll ask for it."

"Well, aren't you a bowl of cherries this morning? Get yourself together. Act professional. So what if she's not the kind of person you want to go have lunch with. That's probably a good thing—I've seen pictures of her. She's not hard on the eyes. The last thing I need is you messing around with a client because she's pretty."

Rian scowled. "Now you're just talking out of your ass. You know I don't do that. If you don't have anything worthwhile to add, I'm going to go."

"Go get some coffee, you mean grouch. It's just for a few days. You can handle this. Laci says hi," he added and Rian grumbled but replied in kind.

His brother had married country superstar Laci McCall, but they'd known her before she'd hit it big and he'd always thought Laci was the best of people. How his brother managed to snag that diamond, he'd never know. Aw, hell, he was just being a surly jerk. Kane and Laci were the real deal and he knew it. If he weren't in such a foul mood, he'd admit that Kane was the luckiest son of a bitch alive.

"Do you need any help with this case?" Kane asked, breaking into Rian's thoughts.

"No, I'm good. Like you said, it's just a few days. I think I can handle Miss Sassy Pants for that amount of time. Anything longer and I might need backup."

"You got it."

Rian clicked off and sighed. His head throbbed and the sunlight stabbing him in the eyeballs wasn't helping any. He needed coffee and he needed it fast. After a quick check on CoCo, he found her dead to the world, lightly snoring and drooling on her pillow. Ha! If he were an asshole, he'd snap a pic of that and post it to social media. Instead he returned to the kitchen to make a pot of coffee.

Of course, as luck would have it, no simple coffee machine around. Just one of those fancy single-cup coffee things that he couldn't make heads or tails of, which meant he had to make do with a glass of iced tea that he managed to make on the fly. It was better than nothing but it didn't compare to the kind of brew he needed to wake up completely.

He was midway through the glass when CoCo stumbled in, bleary-eyed and looking like something the cat dragged in, and he couldn't stop the smirk that followed.

"What are you smiling about?" she asked sourly, going to that fancy machine and popping in a pod on autopilot, because he was certain she could barely see two steps in front of her. "Why are you still here?"

"I told you why I'm here," he answered, more amused than he should be to see her hungover. He saw an opportunity to get some coffee and acted on it. "How about a truce?" he suggested and she stopped to stare at him.

"What are you talking about?"

"Well, we got off on the wrong foot. I'm here to protect you for a handful of days and since there's not much we can do about it, we might as well try to get along. I'll tell you what…you fix me up one of those fancy cups of coffee from your pod machine and I'll forget about what an ungrateful jerk you were to me last night after I saved your bacon. Sound like a deal?" He tacked on a smile for good measure. Time to make lemonade out of lemons. He was good at that.

Except CoCo didn't seem to appreciate his peace offering. She grabbed her coffee and squared her shoulders, the scent of freshly brewed goodness teasing him in the worst way, as she said, "I'm pretty sure they sell coffee at the gas station down the street." Then, blowing on her no doubt delicious coffee, she left him standing there.

Without any coffee.

Well. Hell.

WHAT WAS HE still doing here? She sipped at her coffee, waiting for the caffeine jolt so her brain could function.

She'd thought for sure he would've bailed last night after she'd given him the brush-off. He was like a cursed penny that kept showing up in her purse.

Grabbing her cell, she quickly dialed her father. Time to get to the bottom of this situation. She couldn't have Captain Buzzkill shadowing her every move.

"Babbo," she greeted her father warmly in Italian, "how are you this morning?"

"Malissimo, child," Enzo responded with a heavy sigh that pinched at her earlier pique. "Have you met the man I've hired to watch over you?"

"Ah, yes, actually, I have," she answered, biting her lip, wondering how to break the news that she wanted him to fire Rian. "About that… I don't think he's a good fit for me. I think I'll be fine without a babysitter, *Babbo.* I'm a big girl now. Besides, I doubt we have anything to truly worry about. Perhaps you're just being a little too cautious?"

"Contessa, I will not argue the point with you," Enzo said sternly. Her father only used her given name when he was either fed up or very angry. She may have her father wrapped around her finger but she still shivered when he used that particular tone of voice with her. "Rian Dalton is the best and I trust you in his care. You will do as he says. I have the FBI here with me, working on who is behind this terrorism, but I don't want to worry about you. Am I clear?"

Damn. That didn't go as she'd planned. "But, Babbo… he's such a…" She wrestled with the right word. *Jerk* came to mind but it wasn't just that. He was…unaffected by her in any way. And she found that to be a flaw she couldn't abide. "I'm sure there are plenty of other qualified professionals out there that we can swap him out for. How about I look around and take that load off your shoulders? I would be willing to do that for you."

"Contessa! You will do no such thing. You will abide by my decision. End of discussion."

Should she try again? Under most circumstances she could twist her father into a pretzel to get what she wanted but she sensed this was not one of those times. She'd never heard him so gruff with her. Maybe he was really worried. "Okay, Babbo, I'll stick with Rian," she said glumly. "But I think this is ridiculous. You're going to realize you're overreacting and then I'll get the satisfaction of saying that I was right."

"Perhaps. But until then…you stick with the man I hired and don't give him any of your attitude."

"I'll do my best," she replied, though she couldn't promise. There was something about Rian that rubbed her wrong. Maybe it was the smug smile or the way he didn't bat an eyelash at her looks or her body. She was an expert at wielding sex appeal and most men didn't stand a chance when she put her mind to it but Rian seemed to look right through her. It made her grumpy.

"Grazie, dolcezza," Enzo said with a sigh as he clicked off, and she genuinely wished her father wasn't so burdened by what was happening. She adored her *Babbo*—Italian for daddy—even if she was, admittedly, spoiled rotten as some might say. She tossed her phone onto the bed and reluctantly returned to the kitchen, where Rian was trying to figure out the Keurig coffeemaker. She didn't want to be nice but a handful of days would pass at a snail's pace if they were constantly sniping at each other, so she pushed him aside and fixed him a cup of coffee, thrusting it at him with a glower when it was finished.

"Ah, thank God," Rian said, taking a grateful sip. "That iced tea wasn't going to work. I was ten seconds away from stuffing you in the car and driving to that gas station to get a cup."

"I guess I should be thankful for small favors," she quipped sourly, watching him enjoy his coffee with a critical eye. He was good-looking. In a smug sort of way. "So, apparently my father believes there is a credible threat and that you are the best person for the job in order to keep me safe. Personally, I think this will all blow over and all that will be at risk is my social life. But my father is really stressed and I don't think he's going to change his mind until he gets the all-clear from the FBI, so I guess we're stuck together for the next few days."

"Glad to hear you're coming around," he said from above the rim of his coffee cup. "And for what it's worth…your father is concerned because the threats are becoming more personal. You're his only child. It's only natural for him to want to protect you."

"Of course," she said stiffly. "I'm just saying, this is all pretty over the top. People pop off their mouths all the time. It doesn't mean they actually plan to follow through."

"True. But then, sometimes they do. That's not exactly something you want to take a chance with, you know?"

She nodded, grudgingly ceding the point. "So what now? I'm already bored out of my brain."

"Not my job to entertain you, sweetheart…just to protect you."

"Wrong. If you want to keep me out of harm's way, you'd better find a way to keep me busy. Otherwise,

I'll have to find my own fun, and who knows what that might entail."

"Do you have a death wish or something? This shit is real. Not some game."

She shrugged. "Says you. I think it's all a waste of time. A waste of *my* time. I'm only indulging my father because he's a sweet old man and I adore him."

"Your social calendar will recover," Rian said drily, finishing his coffee and rinsing the cup off to leave in the sink. "But I have more bad news—we're not staying here."

"And just where exactly are we supposed to go?" she queried, her irritation ramping up. "I'm not about to hole up in some hovel if that's what you're thinking."

He laughed. "Don't worry about it, princess. It'll be safe—that's all that matters." He shoved away from the counter and waved her out of the kitchen with a curt command of "Go pack," and she cast a dirty glare his way before returning to her room.

Just where the hell did he plan to take her?

Good God, she hoped it was someplace five-star. She just wasn't in the mood to rough it.

4

HE DIDN'T EXACTLY have a safe house but he knew a hotel that was fairly small and off the beaten path that would serve his purpose. The only problem? It wasn't much to look at. However, that was the point. No one was going to look for an heiress at a two-star hotel that was built in the '70s and hadn't been updated since it was erected. And, okay, maybe he was just a *little* entertained by the idea of subjecting the spoiled brat to something a little less luxurious than she was accustomed to, but it was safe and that was his primary concern.

"Where exactly are you taking me?" she asked, returning with a designer rolling suitcase. "I prefer something along the lines of the Biltmore but I'll settle for the Four Seasons."

He chuckled. "I'll take that under consideration. Are you ready?"

She looked at him with irritation. "I'm standing here with luggage. What do you think that means?"

"All right, then. Let's hit the road."

She grumbled something under her breath but didn't

repeat herself when he gave her a sharp look. They climbed into his Range Rover and took off.

"What are you smiling about?" she asked, suspicious. "You've been the picture of grumpy since the moment we met, yet you're smiling like you just won the lottery."

"What? A man's not allowed to smile in your company?" he asked, smothering his grin when he realized he was borderline gloating in anticipation. Was he being a jerk? Possibly. But she deserved it. He was doing this for all the men out there who'd had the misfortune to snag this girl's eye. No doubt, CoCo had left behind a string of men after she'd had her fun. "Just sit back and enjoy the ride. We're almost there."

She looked out the window with a frown. "Just where exactly are you taking me? This neighborhood doesn't look safe at all. Are you sure you know what you're doing?"

"I know exactly what I'm doing."

"So far, that's debatable."

"Just relax, princess. If there's one thing I know how to do, it's protect overprivileged, spoiled heiresses."

"Exactly how do you get jobs? You have the manners of a pig. Just so you know, so far I haven't been very impressed with your methods. And in case you haven't noticed—people care about what I have to say. One bad review from me and you're finished."

"Have you noticed that you don't have many friends? It might be because you're unbearable to be around."

Her indignant sputter was entertaining. "You don't get to judge me. You're no one. And when this is over my life will go on and yours will be ruined."

Oh, she had balls. "Let me get this straight…you're saying when I'm done protecting your ass, you're going to ruin my career just because I don't jump when you snap your fingers? Hmm, that's not a glowing recommendation for protecting you at all. Maybe I ought to just dump you off at the nearest corner and let you fend for yourself." He barked a laugh at the idea. "You wouldn't last a day."

She shrugged. "You're the one who believes there's a real threat out there, not me. This is all going to blow over. Just wait and see."

"Maybe you're right. But I'm getting paid either way and since you're not the one signing my paycheck just zip your lip and sit tight."

She jerked her gaze away from him with a delicate sniff of annoyance and he had to stop himself from chortling. Why was he baiting her? He'd never acted like this with a client. Not even with the snobbiest, but for some reason he just couldn't shut it down. Her ego needed an ass-whupping in the worst way and he was more than willing to be the one to deliver.

He took the exit ramp and within a block the hotel came into sight. Just as he expected she started to screech.

"Oh, hell no. You're out of your ever-loving mind if you think I'm staying here. It doesn't even look like it has running water or indoor plumbing!"

He put the Range Rover into Park and climbed out with a chuckle. "I promise you there is hot and cold running water. But you're out of luck if you're looking for room service."

She quickly followed, the bee in her bonnet buzzing loudly. "This place is disgusting. I wouldn't let a stray dog sleep here. And you think *I'm* supposed to sleep here? You *are* out of your mind! If I'd wanted to go camping, I would've booked a trip to Yosemite."

"Somehow I can't imagine you camping anywhere."

"That's not the point. I'm not staying here." She stamped her foot. "I told you I would settle for the Four Seasons, not this disgusting edge-of-the-world shack."

"Calm down, princess. It's clean, it's safe and exactly where we need to be right now. No one is going to look for you here."

"Of course not! I feel like I've been kidnapped. I wouldn't stay here if my life depended on it."

"Interesting choice of words. Actually, your life does depend on it. Now come on, let's go."

"I won't and you can't make me," she said, standing her ground with her arms crossed.

"Actually, I can make you. I can throw you over my shoulder and carry you into the hotel room if that's what you prefer. I aim to please." He took a step toward her and she paled.

"You wouldn't dare."

"Try me. You're nothing but a job, princess. And making sure that you are safe is my number-one priority. How you get there or your relative comfort means nothing."

"You're an asshole."

"I've been called worse and by better people. Let's go."

He was almost hoping that she would continue to be a pill but she grabbed her suitcase handle and jerked it toward her, stomping behind him. He could almost feel the heat from her glare burning a hole into his back but as long as she was moving her feet, he didn't care. He made quick work of checking in under false names and then took them straight to the room. He opened the door and saw the problem as soon as she did. He looked at her with a slight apology. "This room used to have two beds."

Her expression withered. "I guess you'll be sleeping on the floor or in the bathtub, then."

"I'm not sleeping in the bathtub," he told her. "We're both adults and if you can keep your hands to yourself, we'll be okay."

She gasped. "As if I would *ever* touch you. I'd rather die first."

"Don't be so dramatic," he said with a short scowl. "Besides, you're not my type, honey."

"Like I believe that," she muttered. "I saw the way you looked at me when we first met."

"That was an act," he said, happy to throw a bucket of water on her smug comment. "I prefer my women to be a lot less *spawn of the devil*, more of the human variety."

"Ha-ha. Yes, well, women bought by the hour tend to be more agreeable." She cast a disparaging look around the room. "I'll bet you bring your girls here. Seems appropriate for that kind of commerce."

He narrowed his gaze. "Careful, princess. One of these days your mouth is going to overload your ass."

She ignored his warning. "I can't believe you brought me to this place and now you think you're going to sleep in the same bed with me. Unbelievable. Maybe I'll just sleep in the car."

"Negative. You stay where I can keep an eye on you. That's the whole point of coming to a place like this. It might not look like much but from a defensive standpoint it's pretty solid. A place like the Biltmore or the

Four Seasons is a logistical nightmare. Too many people coming and going and it's way too easy to pretend to be someone you're not. Here, there's no room service—which means no one is coming to the door that hasn't been invited and all points of entry are easily watched. So, it's not the lap of luxury but it will serve its purpose."

"I can't believe this is happening," she muttered, but something he said must've made sense because she stopped arguing even if she added, "I'm still not sleeping with you. You can take the floor." She moved past him and closed herself in the bathroom.

"Just so you know, the idea of sleeping next to you isn't high on my priority list, either," he called out and she barked an incredulous laugh, mocking him.

As if he'd want to snuggle up to that spitting cobra? He'd rather chew off his own foot.

This was going to be the hardest he'd ever worked for a dollar, that was for damn sure.

THAT MAN HAD lost his mind if he thought he was going to climb into her bed as if he had a right to. She'd rejected hotter guys than him and he'd best remember that she was a catch! She sat on the closed toilet lid, quietly fuming. He had to be the single most annoying, rude jerk that she'd ever met—and that was saying a lot because she circulated in some pretty elite circles filled with self-important blowhards. At this rate, she was ready to surrender to whoever was threatening her family if it meant that she no longer had to put up with Rian Dalton. Who did he think he was? She had some of the richest, most eligible bachelors on two continents running after her and he had the gall to turn his nose up at her? That man was not only rude but an idiot, as well.

So what was she going to do, sit in the bathroom all day? No. He was not going to chase her off. She splashed some water on her face and then exited the bathroom with her chin held high. "I find it hard to believe that this is the best that you can find as a safe house. You can't tell me that you bring politicians and other celebrities here to this awful place." The slow, lazy smile told her exactly what she needed to know, and she clenched her fists as she howled. "You're torturing me on purpose!"

But even as he didn't rightly deny it, he didn't admit it, either. "I find it important to adjust accordingly. This was the best place I could find that was suited to the situation," he said as if she weren't smarter than that, and she called him on it.

"Bullshit. You picked this place because it sucks and you don't like me. Do you think I'm stupid?"

"Not at all. I think you're very smart. But you're also a pain in the ass. Did I pick this place because I thought it might annoy you? *Maybe.* But my original reasons stand. It's a safe place. Deal with it."

"Deal with it? Deal with *what*? The fact that there are probably more cockroaches in this place than there are actual *people*? We are in the middle of nowhere, I'm not sure when these bedsheets were cleaned last and I'm fairly certain people have probably been murdered in their sleep here. Why would I feel *safe* here?"

"I doubt anyone has been murdered in this room."

"And that's supposed to make me feel better? I swear to God, if my father wasn't wholeheartedly convinced that you were the only one who could do this job, I would walk out the door right now and gladly never see you again."

"Well, I guess I should be thankful for small favors. One thing, though, are you going to be this screechy the whole time? If so, I will need to invest in earplugs. Your voice is grating."

Grating? She sputtered. "You have a lot of nerve. I don't know if I should be impressed by your decided lack of common sense or if I should feel pity for you because you're an overwhelming idiot."

He snapped his fingers with a smile. "Earplugs it is."

She growled. The man was insufferable. "This room is about to lose its murder-free status because I'm going to kill *you* in your sleep."

"Careful, making threats like that is a felony. I'd hate to have to arrest you. Although, you sitting in jail would definitely be a safe place. But I can't promise that the accommodations are superior to what we have right here."

"You wouldn't dare."

"Princess, you'll find that I dare much. Keep pushing and you'll find out just how far I'm willing to go."

There was something about the way he held her gaze that sent a dangerous thrill arcing through her nerve endings. There was no pushing him around—no bulldozing him. Men crumbled when she pushed. Not Rian. He not only pushed back, he dared her to push harder. There was something electric dancing between them even if neither wanted to admit it. And that stubborn mouth had the most sensual lips she'd ever seen. So he wasn't hard on the eyes, she grudgingly admitted, finding it hard to pull her gaze away when she realized she'd been staring a little too long. Rian would be the perfect guy to have angry, I-hate-you sex with. If she were into that kind of thing. "So if there's no room service, how exactly do you plan to feed me?" she finally asked.

He pulled a brown square package from his backpack and tossed it at her. She caught it in confusion. "What the hell is this?"

"That, my dear, is a military-issue MRE. I think it's meat loaf. Not bad but not great, either. I don't want to oversell it."

She dropped the package as if it were made of poison and it landed on the floor with a dull thud. "Are you kidding me? Those things have, like, three thousand calories. I can't eat that."

"They fill the belly. I suppose if you get hungry enough you'll dig in."

"You can't be serious. We're not at war. There is no reason why I should have to eat something meant for soldiers in the field. And I don't believe you eat these, either. If you had a steady diet of MREs, you'd be fat as a tick."

He rubbed his belly. "I guess I just have a fast metabolism."

There was no winning with this man. She threw her hands up. "I guess I'll starve. And when you return me to my father, starving and near death because I haven't had any food or water, something tells me he won't be hot to write you a check."

He sighed dramatically. "You are the biggest pain. Fine, I'll go get you something to eat, but I'm talking burgers and fries, not some fancy French froufrou stuff. Got it?"

She supposed that was a victory of some sort. "It'll do for now. But if that's how you eat normally, your arteries must be clogged with gunk."

"Don't worry about my arteries—they're just fine."

"Are you always this much of a jerk with all your clients?" she asked. "Because you have terrible manners. I can't imagine you're saving all of that just for me."

"How about you, princess? Your manners aren't exactly great, either. I would ask how you have any friends at all but then you're rich, so that probably helps. People can put up with a lot if they're getting perks. Do you hand out Coach bags for the ones that hang around the longest?"

She drew back, stung. "That's ridiculous. You don't know me and you certainly don't know what my friends are like."

"Oh, I have a pretty good idea. Don't you remember I watched you all night last night? I hate to break it to you but I'm willing to bet you don't have any true friends. All those people were doing was trashing your house—excuse me, it's not even your house—trashing your *mother's* house. Doesn't that bother you?"

"They weren't trashing the house," she disagreed hotly. "And besides, we have a cleaning company coming in to pick up in the morning. My mom will never know."

"That's not the point. It's not your place to trash. If you are throwing a raging party at a house—pick your own."

She blinked back sudden tears. "Excuse me, I don't think it's your job to lecture me. You don't know my family dynamics so butt out."

"You're right. And I don't care about your family dynamics. All I know is that someone is out there pretty pissed off at your family and looking to take it out on anyone they can get their hands on. But you have to wonder what is it you guys did to piss someone off that bad."

"Who said we pissed anyone off? My father is a very rich, influential man. Sometimes people are just envious of his success."

He shrugged. "Perhaps. Or maybe your dad stepped on too many people on his way to the top."

"Look, you don't get to talk about my dad that way. You don't know him. He is the nicest man you'll ever meet. He would give you the shirt off his back if you needed it. But he shouldn't be made to apologize for his success. He worked his ass off to get where he is right now and it's shady people who think that they're entitled to what someone else has that has put us in this position."

Her heated answer surprised him enough to soften a little. "All right, you've made your point. All I'm saying is that you're not making anything easier with your bad attitude."

"And it's my job to make your job easier?"

"Maybe if you weren't so difficult, people would be more interested in helping you."

She cocked her head at him. "And by people, do you mean you? Because I'm not looking for your approval."

"Whatever, princess. All I'm saying is… Hell, forget it. You can't hear anything that you don't want to hear anyway." He went to the door. "Stay here. I'm going to get your food. Don't leave."

And then he was gone. For a long moment she just stared at the door, his words banging around in her head. Why did she care what he thought? He was no one. But knowing that he thought so little of her, that all he saw was a spoiled heiress, pinched her hard. She was more than that. And she hadn't always been this way. Growing up for the first part of her life in rural Italy, she'd been like a lot of other girls. It wasn't until her parents split up and she had to travel between two different continents that things changed.

It sounded like more poor rich-girl problems but no one knew what it was like to be raised by nannies, rarely seeing her parents. Her mother was never around, always too busy finding the next man of the hour to bother with a little girl. She lost herself to a moment of self-pity. No one understood—and that included Rian Dalton. Not that it mattered. She didn't care what he thought.

5

STOP WITH THE DEBATES, he chastised himself. It was unhealthy and unprofessional—but he couldn't seem to keep his mouth shut. She brought out the worst in him. Maybe he ought to call Kane and have him take over. But even as the sensible thought flitted across his mind, he couldn't actually commit. He didn't want anyone else handling this case.

Maybe because giving up would feel like a failure, or maybe it was because of something else, but he just wasn't ready to let go. And the fact that CoCo was calling him on his bullshit was something that he hadn't expected. Yeah, she was smart. She'd seen right through the fact that he was deliberately baiting her. Sure, the place was safe—he wouldn't lie about that—but there were other places he could've picked that were just as safe but not as squalid.

The thing about the bed, though, that'd come as a shock. In the past when he'd used this place, there'd been two full beds. But it'd been a while since he'd come around and the management must've decided to spruce things up. He could try to switch rooms but he couldn't give up the strategic position, and he wasn't about to take chances with CoCo's life even if she did irritate the shit out of him.

He made quick work of finding a burger joint, ordering enough food to last them for the night, and then returned to the hotel. This time, he told himself, he wasn't going to let her get under his skin. He was a professional and he was going to start acting like one. With a quick look around to make sure that nobody was watching him, he let himself into the room.

Time to start fresh. "Look, since we have to work together for the next couple of days, how about we call a truce? I won't needle you and you won't needle me and we'll get along just fine." He handed her a bag of burger and fries.

She accepted the food offering with a small nod. "I guess that'll be okay. But this place sucks. Surely we can go somewhere else, somewhere less third-world country."

"Not tonight. Maybe tomorrow. Right now we need to hole up and make sure that the place is secure."

She made an exasperated sound, wanting to slap him silly right in that too-hot-for-his-own-good face. "Enough with the dire warnings of imminent death. What an enormous wet blanket you are. Do you realize how many times somebody has threatened my dad's life? People are crazy. But nothing has ever happened to him and we're going to be fine."

"Have you read any of the threats that have come his way?" he asked.

She shook her head. "My dad doesn't let me see those things but I know he's been threatened before. The thing is, when you have a lot of money, you have a lot of enemies. And it's not because you did anything specific, it's just because some people with less hate those who have more."

"Sometimes," he agreed. "But sometimes they also have a reason. Do you think there's any reason why your dad might be targeted?"

"No. This is the work of someone who's just crazy. I'm sure of it."

But Rian wasn't so sure. Enzo had to believe this was a credible threat to bring in the big hitters. "I can tell you that the FBI doesn't get involved unless it's a real threat. I think your dad is right in keeping you out of harm's way. You are an easy target. If whoever is threatening him got a hold of you, all the power would be in their hands."

Obviously she hadn't thought of it that way. "But I don't understand who would hate him so much that they would do this. I don't understand it at all. My dad makes shoes, for crying out loud. It's not like he's trading in state secrets."

"How do you know? A shoe business would make a great front."

She hit him with a dark look.

He raised his hands in mock surrender. "I'm not calling your dad anything. I'm just playing devil's advocate."

"Well, stop. My dad is an honorable man."

"I apologize. I'm not trying to say anything bad against your dad. I'm just trying to put together the pieces of the puzzle."

"It's not your job to figure out anything. Your job is to keep me safe."

She had a point, but did she have to be so bitchy

about it? "Yeah, I hear you. Loud and clear." It was his fault for thinking he and CoCo could engage in a civil conversation. He gestured to her cheeseburger. "Eat your burger. I'm not heading back out just because you let your food go cold."

They ate in silence—which surprised him because he didn't think that CoCo had the ability to remain quiet. Either way it was a welcome respite.

SHE HADN'T MEANT to be rude but his comment about her father rubbed her the wrong way. Maybe because she'd worried herself that her father had done something to bring this trouble on their heads. She didn't know his business practices but she assumed he was an honorable man because she hated to think of him any other way. The fact that Rian had thrown the question on the table had only served to bring up her own misgivings.

"How did you get into this line of work?" she asked, needing something to keep her from obsessing about things she couldn't control. The close quarters were bad enough but being locked in a room with Rian was doing confusing things to her insides. "I mean, it doesn't seem like something you just fall into on a whim."

"Oh, is this story hour? Now are we gonna share about each other's lives and sing 'Kumbaya'?"

She drew back with a bristle. "Look, I'm just trying to make the time pass. If you want to be a jerk about it, fine. We can stare at the walls and watch the cockroaches to pass the time."

That seemed to knock some sense into him as he had the decency to look regretful. "Sorry, I'm not used to you being friendly. I didn't recognize it as a genuine attempt at small talk."

"See? That's what I'm talking about. I try to be nice and then you go and say something mean and then it starts all over again. Can't we get along for ten minutes?"

"Yeah, sure. Sorry. Let me switch gears for a minute." He wiped his mouth and acted as if he was indeed switching a gear in his head. "All right, what do you want to know? How did I get into this business? My brother, Kane, and I started it up when we realized there were plenty of people out there who would pay through the nose for a little protection. We figured we had the skills—former military, special skills training—and we decided to make it work for us. It was either that or spend the rest of our lives in therapy for PTSD issues. This seemed like the better option."

"You've been in open combat?" she asked, surprised and a little impressed. "Do you have any scars?"

"Mental or physical?"

She shrugged. "Either."

"Both. But like I said, therapy just didn't seem like it was gonna work out. I like to shoot things. And in our line of work we get the opportunity to do that. And get paid well for it, so it's a win-win."

"So, you and your brother do this together? Is your brother like you?"

"No." He paused to grin. "He's not as nice."

At that she laughed. "Wow. Thanksgiving dinner around your table must be pretty fun."

"Yeah, well, we're not big on the holiday scene. Neither of us make a big deal out of that stuff because we never really had it growing up." A moment passed between them before he pulled himself out of his own thoughts to switch his attention back to her. "What do you do for fun when you're not out there playing into the stereotype?"

"And what stereotype would that be?" she asked drily. "And here I thought we were off to a good start. You just don't know how to be nice, do you?"

"Sorry, sorry. You're right. I can't seem to watch my mouth around you. Tell me what you do for fun."

"I do whatever I want to do." Damn it, now she was the one being defensive. But what could she say? She did love her life. Might as well own it. "I shop. I party." That's what he expected her to say, anyway. As if he would believe her if she told him that she actually wanted to design shoes like her father. Besides, that was private. She wasn't going to share that with Rian and run the risk of being mocked. "This was a stupid idea, to chitchat. We obviously have nothing in common."

"Don't get your panties twisted. We just seem to set each other off for some reason. I'm interested in knowing more about you—the real you. I'm listening if you want to try again."

She eyed him with suspicion. "Seriously? You're not just saying that?"

"I don't say a thing I don't mean. Go ahead, tell me something interesting about yourself."

CoCo took a moment to think, then said, "Well, I speak fluent Italian, decent French and a tiny bit of Russian."

His brows rose. "That is impressive. Benefit of being shuttled between parents who live on opposite continents?"

"Mostly. But European school systems are different than here in the States. It's just natural for most kids to speak more than one language. I don't want to sound superior anything but the European school system is much more rigorous."

"Makes sense. Although if I was required to learn more than one language I probably would've failed high school. English was hard enough." He chuckled. "But that's actually kind of cool that you're fluent in so many other languages."

She smiled. "It comes in handy when ordering in fancy restaurants. I'm usually the only one who knows what I'm actually ordering."

He laughed. "Are you the designated orderer when you go to restaurants with your friends?"

She nodded. "Yes. But I don't mind. I like being helpful when I can."

That must've amazed him. "Tell me something else about yourself that would surprise me."

"Why?" Were they actually having a decent conversation? She wasn't sure if this was good or bad. Keeping a professional distance might help with the annoying flits of excitement tickling her stomach each time she caught him smiling. He had nice, kissable lips when he wasn't being a colossal toad. "I mean, don't get me wrong, I like that we're not trying to kill each other right now but I'm not quite sure why you're suddenly being so nice."

He sighed, stretching out his legs as he confessed, "Look, I was a jerk when we first met. There's something about you that gets under my skin. I grew up really poor. I'm talking the kind of poverty that no one likes to think about. It makes it hard to see all these people who have so much act so crappy to their fellow human beings. I've always believed that if you have extra you should give a little extra. But that doesn't seem to be the prevailing attitude around here. Los Angeles is a whole other world and not a very generous one from what I can see."

"I try to donate when I can. I mean, I don't do it as much as I should but I have a few charities that I like to donate to."

"See, that's what I'm talking about. You're an heiress and you never have to worry about where your next meal is coming from, but when I was growing up I went days without food. My old man was a bastard drunk, and a mean one at that. If it weren't for my older brother—well, let's just say I probably wouldn't be here today. Being hungry is something kids should never have to experience. There are basic rights a human being should have and food is one of them."

CoCo didn't know how to respond. She'd never gone a day in her life knowing the pangs of hunger. "I'm sorry that you had to go through that. You're right, every kid deserves food. But that's really no reason to take it out on me just because I didn't experience the same kind of childhood. I don't mean to ruin this nice moment we're having but you came at me with an attitude from the moment we met. And it wasn't really fair. You didn't know me from anyone and you judged me."

"True," he admitted. "However, I hate to say this but I wasn't too far off the mark. I might've come off a little brusque but you were worse. What's that say about you?"

"It says that I don't like strangers crashing my party," she answered coolly. "If I was nice to every single person who just randomly walked up to me, who knows who I'd be inviting into my life? I might not know what it's like to live in extreme poverty but you don't know what it's like to live with extreme wealth. People can't be trusted most times. Your inner circle becomes smaller and smaller and it's out of necessity, not because you don't like people. You never know who wants to rip you off."

He was openly confused. "If that was the case, why did you have a house filled with people that you didn't even know? You can't tell me that all those people who came to your party are your personal friends. I guarantee half of those people were only there because they wanted to say they'd attended a CoCo Abelli party. I hate to break it to you, princess, but you have a reputation and it isn't a pretty one."

She blinked. "And what is that supposed to mean?"

"Why do you think the paparazzi follow you? It's because you're always getting yourself into trouble. Getting drunk, wardrobe malfunctions, partying too hard… it paints a picture."

"It's not my fault that photographers follow me around," she said bitterly, embarrassed. "What if someone with a camera was always in your face every time that you went out? You can't tell me that you haven't made mistakes, maybe drank a little too much or whatever with friends. I make a mistake and it ends up all over the tabloids. That's not my fault."

"I'm sorry I don't buy the 'poor me' routine. You put yourself in these positions and they capitalize on them. You say I don't know what it's like to have extreme wealth, you're right. I don't. But I know for certain I wouldn't be out getting drunk and giving the paparazzi so much to work with."

"You don't understand," she said, shaking her head. "There's an expectation and understanding that if you run in certain circles you're going to have to host certain parties."

"Screw those circles. Doesn't sound like the kind of circle I'd want to be in."

"It's easy for you to judge because you don't live my life."

"Absolutely. It's also easy for me to see that what you're doing isn't healthy. You're too close to the situation, you can't see that you're screwing up your life."

She didn't have to listen to this. Or did she? Where was she supposed to go? She was stuck in a tiny room. "Okay, story hour is over. Somehow we can't even have a basic conversation without insulting one another. How about we just spend the next couple of days refraining from saying a single word to one another. Sound like a plan?"

"I have one final thing to say about this, because it seems like no one else in your life has the balls to tell you what you don't want to hear. Anyone who would encourage you to get shit-faced drunk or high on pills doesn't care about you—you're simply the entertainment for the night. So you have money… No one says you have to act like an asshole. You could be giving. You could be generous. You could make lives better for other people. But instead you spend your time thinking only of yourself and how everything in the world affects you. I hate to break it to you, sweetheart, but the world is bigger than the circle you're occupying."

6

WHY COULDN'T HE KEEP his damn mouth shut? Things had been going smoothly—and then he had to go and lay all that truth on her like a load of bricks. It wasn't his job to be her Jiminy Cricket. If she didn't have a conscience about how she spent her life or how she frittered away her blessings, that was her problem. So why did it bother him so much that she refused to see the truth? He didn't know her, not really. True, all he knew about her was from the tabloids and maybe that was his fault for only caring to look that deep, but it drove him crazy when people did so little for their fellow man.

"You know, I've seen people with so little to their names that they could carry everything they owned on their person, and yet they'll be the first to offer you something if you need it. And then I've worked with people who owned yachts and mansions and throw lavish parties for their dogs but wouldn't drop a dollar into a collection cup. There's something wrong with the world when that's okay."

"Not everyone has to live by your definition of generosity," she shot back hotly. "No one has to toe the line because you say so."

"Maybe not but I think the world would be better off if they did. Every year I donate a big chunk of my income to charitable causes because I know what it's like to go home hungry, to be cold, to wear clothes two sizes too small. My brother used to dig through a trash can behind a restaurant so that we could have food. Your idea of roughing it is staying at a place like this. When I was a kid this would've been the Taj Mahal. It's all about perspective, I guess. It's just my opinion, but I think you have a screwed-up sense of what's right and what's wrong in this world, princess. So yeah, my judgment comes on pretty strong because I've lived it."

"But it's not my fault that you were poor," she said, blinking back tears. "Do you treat everyone who has money like this? All of your clients are rich. Do you treat them like dirt simply because they have more money than you?"

"No, of course not," he said, frustrated. "But for some reason with you, it bothers me. It bothers me a lot. I know you could be a better person."

What had he just said? He needed a roll of duct tape to stick across his mouth because he was saying all sorts of loopy things. "*Arrrgh!* You're right, this was a bad idea. We shouldn't have started this conversation. I'm sorry I got sucked into it. From now on no more talking of personal stuff. Let's just keep things superficial and we'll be cool. Yeah?"

"Fine," she agreed grumpily. "I'm going to shower." She scooted from the bed and disappeared into the bathroom and he was glad. He needed time to get his head on straight. How could things disintegrate so quickly between them? There was something about her that twisted him sideways—and maybe what bothered him the most was that he couldn't stop looking at her. Everything about her represented something he didn't believe in but his eyes sure liked what he saw. He couldn't seem to stop noticing the way the slender column of her neck joined the soft flesh of her shoulders, and how her eyes lit up with passion when she was putting him in his place. It was stupid and he didn't like the way his heart jammed to a foreign beat whenever his gaze strayed to her ass or her breasts.

For one, he shouldn't even be looking at her like that—he never messed around with clients, that was bad business. For two, there was nothing about CoCo that encouraged a casual hookup and he didn't have the time or the interest for anything beyond a superficial good time.

He fell back on the bed, listening as the shower started. Great. Now he was thinking of her naked. He rubbed his eyes, trying to remove the images his imagination gleefully threw at him. She had a smoking-hot body—there were plenty of pictures on the internet of CoCo in a bikini—and she had that European mystique coupled with a California sass that was hard to forget about. As if he needed another complication, his cock tried to get in on the action by suddenly tenting his jeans. Good gravy, that's all he needed—CoCo seeing that he was rock hard. That would horrify them both. He pushed at his cock with an irritated growl. *Settle down, not gonna happen.* He popped up from the bed and gathered their trash from lunch and stuffed it into the small wastebasket, then slid the chain across the door before taking his gun and double-checking his rounds. He hated to admit it but CoCo was right—they might die from boredom in this hotel room.

He'd never been so out of control of his emotions before. He knew how to keep it together under most circumstances but CoCo seemed to tip him on his head without even trying. If he'd been thinking clearly, he would've holed up with some puzzle books or something, anything to pass the time. But he'd been so hell-bent on taking CoCo someplace that would make her miserable that he hadn't actually thought things through. That was dangerous. He'd done screwed the pooch. Kane would slap him silly if he knew. Okay, so time to get back to basics. They'd cool it here for the night and then tomorrow they'd leave for a different place. Maybe the Ojai ranch. When his brother married Laci, she'd come with a nice spread in Ojai and they often used the ranch when they wanted to get out of the city. It was remote enough without being in the sticks and close enough to Los Angeles to be convenient. It was far nicer than this place for sure.

But first, he had to see if it was available.

He dialed Kane. "Hey, man," he said once Kane answered. "Is anyone at the ranch right now?"

"Yeah, sorry. While Laci is off tour we're letting her hairdresser and costume designer stay there. Why?"

Disappointment colored his voice. "I was hoping to use it for a few days."

"Sorry, man. What's wrong?"

"Nothing," he said a bit too quickly and Kane caught it.

"Let's pretend that we went a couple of rounds where you continue to deny anything is wrong so we can actually get to the point and find out what's really happening."

He didn't need to hear what he knew his brother would say so he cut it short. "Nothing. I just wanted to get out of the city."

"You can come here," Kane offered. "Laci and I are going to Montana for a few weeks. You could hole up here if you want."

Head back to Woodsville? Not a chance. Just because Kane and Laci had built a love nest on the Bradford ranch didn't mean that Rian had an itch to do the same. He loved them all but he didn't love Woodsville. Too many bad memories.

"I'm good," he told Kane. "Enjoy Montana."

"Well, if you change your mind, the spare key is under the pump."

"I won't but thanks."

"Suit yourself. See you in a few weeks, little brother."

Rian clicked off and sighed, wondering what he was going to do. *Just keep your hands to yourself and everything will be just fine,* he told himself.

Should be easy enough, right?

CoCo STEPPED GINGERLY into the tiny shower, grimacing as she glanced around, trying not to imagine how many germs and cooties were bouncing around just waiting to climb onto her skin. A tiny sliver of soap rested on the ledge and she stared unhappily at the obviously used toiletry. Her revulsion nearly sent her screaming from the shower into a full-fledged diva meltdown until she remembered what Rian had told her about his childhood. Had he really eaten from the trash? Was he just saying that for effect?

She didn't know him at all but she sensed that he'd been totally honest. Maybe it was the way he'd seemed slightly ashamed once the hot words had escaped his mouth, or maybe the way his eyes had flashed with rage at the indignity, but it'd felt real. He probably hadn't meant to share so much, she realized. That's probably not something she'd want to share, either.

Gritting her teeth, she picked up the soap and, after rinsing it thoroughly, lathered up. It smelled like straight lye and would probably dry her skin to paper but at least she'd be clean. If she'd known they were going to hole up in hell, she would've showered at her mom's place before leaving. She'd mistakenly assumed he was going to take her to the Four Seasons or some other suitably luxurious hotel. She cast her gaze around the sorry bathroom and shuddered at how off the mark she'd been.

The fact that he'd done this to her on purpose, perhaps to teach her a lesson, really burned. It was hard not to fall headlong into a temper tantrum but she held it back—only because she didn't want to further fuel his clichéd expectations of her. She hated that he thought so little of her but there wasn't much she could say that would change his mind because she hadn't really done much to crow about. But why should she feel guilty about that? Was it her fault that she'd been born to money and he hadn't? Why was it okay for him to punish her for something that had been out of her control?

She scrubbed a little harder. He didn't have the right to judge her for anything. So what if she couldn't remember the last time she'd made a sizable donation to her favorite charity? Her father made giant donations every year to a number of causes in the family name. So, in a way, she'd donated, too. Oh, that was flimsy, even by her standards. The fight evaporated and she was left with a black hole of sadness that felt familiar even as she tried to ignore it.

All her life she'd tried to fight that gnawing ache inside her, and it felt a lot like this. She ducked under the spray and tried to stop sinking further but Rian's words weighed on her. No one expected anything from her because she rarely mattered. Even though she adored her father, it wasn't as if he'd actually had a hand in raising her. She'd had countless nannies to do that. And her mother hadn't been much better.

CoCo had been an afterthought, a pretty extension of the family name, brought out at parties and then returned to the nursery when it suited them. Tears burned under her lids. Why was she crying? What was wrong with her? It was Rian's fault. Everything had been fine until Rian had shown up sowing seeds of unhappiness and discontent. Hadn't she had a blast at her party last night? Yeah, up until that dickhead Drake had decided to push things too far. Well, that was an isolated incident. Before that, everything had been peachy. So the problem was clearly Rian.

CoCo shut off the water and snatched the scratchy towel from the rack. She wrapped the towel around her with a grimace as it scraped against her tender skin and then she emerged from the bathroom in a cloud of steam. The towel was barely larger than a hand towel and hardly covered her but she didn't care. If Rian wanted to be her babysitter, then he could do it on her terms. She was going out tonight.

"What are you doing?" he asked, sitting up straight as an arrow, his eyes wide. "Why aren't you dressed?"

"You know what, this is bullshit. I don't want to sit

in this dinky, gross, completely unsuitable hotel for the next few days with nothing but your judgment to keep me occupied so I'm going out tonight. If you want to babysit me, fine, then you're going to have to do it while I'm having some fun."

"Like hell you are. Now get some clothes on," he growled and she taunted him with a smile.

What are you going to do about it?

He shot her with a warning look. "I mean it. Don't test me, CoCo."

"What? You don't like me in my towel? Is there something wrong?" she asked coyly, enjoying the sudden flush in his cheeks as she toyed with him. This was the way to rattle him, she realized with a spurt of enjoyment. He'd brought her to this place as a punishment and, well, she had ways of punishing him, too. "I wonder what would happen if I did…this?" Then in a deliberate move she dropped the towel to the floor, and she smiled as she watched Rian's eyes nearly pop out of his head.

That's right, Rian Dalton…two can play games but only one is going to win.

Me.

7

OH, HELL, SAVE ME.

Rian loved women of all shapes and sizes but CoCo had a body that made him forget about all others. And she was using it against him. There was only one way to handle the situation and it was with swift action. He rose from the bed and scooped up the towel, going straight to her with purpose while she backed away, smiling in a way that made his groin tighten, but he wasn't going to let his dick run the show. He tried to keep his gaze on her face but, damn, he was only human, and those breasts were something of a national treasure.

"Like what you see?" she asked.

"Seen 'em before," he said evenly, impressed that he was able to keep his voice calm. "It's not like you haven't put them on display before." Then he roughly wrapped the towel around her, relieved as hell when he could no longer see those luscious pink nipples pointing straight at him, begging him to suck and nip. God help him, he was only human. "That's not going to work on me, CoCo," he told her, and she just laughed because she didn't believe him. Who could blame her? He was practically pinning her to the wall with his boner. "Now get dressed and don't do that again."

"Well, I suppose we could stay in…" CoCo said suggestively and his jaw tightened. "What? Did you take a vow of celibacy like a Tibetan monk?"

"No. I just don't mess around with clients."

"Hmm, well, that sounds terribly boring. Fine, then, if we're not going to *mess around*, as you put it, then I'm going back to my original plan. I'm going out."

"You're staying put. You can watch some boob tube." The moment the careless words fell from his mouth he cringed. He couldn't have picked a sorrier choice of words given the fact that he'd just gotten an eyeful of the most amazing breasts he'd ever laid eyes on. Now she was going to think he was obsessed with her boobs. Even if he was, that was private information and not something he was likely to come out and admit. "You know what I mean," he said, gesturing to the old television. He wasn't even sure it worked. *Please, God, let there be cable.*

"Sorry, not a big *boob tube* fan," she said with a saucy grin. "I'm going out. You can either come or stay. Your choice but I am not staying in this hovel a minute longer than I have to."

He started to shoot her down but she dropped that damn towel again and he lost all the thoughts in his head. He glared as she scooped up her clothes and returned to the bathroom, knowing full well she was giving him a long, hard look at her ass, and then shut the door with barely contained laughter.

That woman, he was fairly certain, was made by the devil to tempt him into throwing away his career.

And right now, he was having a hard time remembering why he made it a rule to never sleep with clients.

Because at the moment...staying in and getting to know each other a helluva lot better was beginning to have a ton of appeal.

That was a problem.

"Fine!" he bit out. "But only for a little while. We're not staying out late, you hear me?"

"We'll stay out for as long as I want."

"You're really pushing my buttons, princess," he snarled and she laughed because she already knew there was nothing he could do about it. He had no doubt that if he refused her demand to go out, she'd make his life miserable by trying to seduce him, and in the current state he was in, she damn well might succeed, so he had no choice but to take her out.

Well, this was a fine mess.

How in the hell had CoCo gotten the upper hand in this? He shifted his hips to adjust the raging erection in his pants and he smothered a groan. He looked down at the bulge and muttered, "Yeah, it's all your fault. Thanks a lot."

"Be ready in about ten minutes," she called out in a singsong voice, and his gut clenched again. This was madness but it was either give in or put out.

He wasn't sure which would be worse for his state of mind at this point.

CoCo FELT A RUSH of feminine power. Rian wasn't so immune as he liked to put on. He wanted her. She'd been around enough men to know when they were into her. She'd been playing with men since she turned fifteen and had since honed her skills, cutting her teeth on European and American men alike. Rian Dalton was no match for her. Why hadn't she gone this route in the first place?

She carefully applied her makeup and dressed in a tiny black dress that hugged her curves and dipped low in the back and she grinned, knowing Rian would be staring at her ass all night. Good. Let him stare. Let him hunger. Maybe if he was lucky, she would let him cop a feel. She'd known that he wouldn't compromise his integrity for a roll in the hay so she'd been pretty assured that he'd give in to her demand to go out, which he had. Men were so predictable.

"Just what are you wearing, woman?" Rian demanded, staring hard at her dress. She couldn't quite tell if he liked it or was appalled. "There's hardly enough to cover half your body. You can't go out like that."

She laughed. "You like it? It's one of my favorites."

"No, I don't like it," he answered, but his gaze said otherwise. Her skin heated at the hunger she saw building behind his eyes. "Don't you have a jacket or something you could put on over it? The last thing I need is to fend off a legion of horny guys once they catch a glimpse of you in that thing."

"Aw, how cute. Would you defend my honor?" she asked demurely and he snorted. She rolled her eyes and grabbed her purse. "And here I thought I was seeing the gentleman in you. Whatever happened to all that Southern charm I hear about? I guess that saying that Southern men know how to treat a lady is totally false."

"When I see a lady I'll let you know," he retorted and she glared. He gestured to her dress. "Just sayin'."

"It's couture," she told him with a sniff. The man wouldn't know high fashion if it bit him in that cute butt.

"It's the size of a postage stamp."

"Not the point. Humor me…what do you really think?"

He hesitated and for a second she thought he might fall back on a smart-ass quip but instead he shocked her with an honest answer. "You look damn fine and you know it." It looked as if his answer had cost him by the way his mouth tightened and his gaze darted, but she warmed at the admission just the same. "Can we go now? Let's just get this over with," he growled and she had to suppress a shiver at the way his voice danced on her vertebrae.

Maybe it wasn't such a good idea to toy with him like this. It seemed she wasn't entirely immune to him, either.

It was still a little early to hit the clubs so she suggested cocktails first. "I know a cute little place on West Fifth Street, not too big, where we can get a drink and appetizers before we hit the clubs. I'll even do you a solid and buy the first round."

"I'm not drinking and you shouldn't, either," he said, raining on her parade. "This ain't a vacation."

"C'mon, stop being such a stick-in-the-mud. One drink isn't going to hurt anyone. Besides, you look like you could use a beer or something."

He didn't disagree, which was a point in her favor. "One drink and that's it," he finally relented and she silently crowed with victory.

"Sure. One drink," she agreed, though she had no plans to stick to that promise. "I think you'll like this place. It has a real laid-back atmosphere but it's still classy."

"Fine." He exhaled as if he were being dragged to

hell and back for the sake of the job and she decided that they were going to have a good time, whether he liked it or not.

She snuck a sidelong glance at him and couldn't stop the smile even as that tiny tingle in the pit of her stomach also rang with a warning. Rian wasn't like the guys she was used to hanging around. He didn't play games, he was a straight shooter and he didn't hold back when he believed something was wrong.

But there was something else that she sensed about him—and it was that little bell ringing in her head that she knew she ought to heed.

Rian had that certain something about him that said when he took a woman to his bed, she didn't leave until he was thoroughly finished with her.

She sucked in a sharp breath as her heart skipped a beat. Rian was probably a stallion in the bedroom. She pictured all that hard muscle wrapped around his lean frame and arousal warmed her belly.

"Are you okay?" he asked, shooting her a concerned look. "You got all flushed."

"I'm fine," she assured him quickly with a believable lie. "Just happy to be getting away from this hotel."

Suddenly, she wished Rian would've called her bluff. Maybe staying in wouldn't have been so bad after all…

8

Enzo rubbed at his chest, trying to ease the ache that seemed to get more intense each time he thought of the situation facing his family. He had no idea who was threatening his family and his business but the fact that the threats had become more violent frightened him more than he wanted to admit.

"Here are your designs for the upcoming *Lusso* line," said Georgina, his personal secretary, as she entered his office. Young and pretty, Georgina was also sharp as a tack and kept his business running smoothly. She was also his lover. She frowned as she noted his distress. "What's wrong?"

He sighed and pushed away the paperwork that he'd been staring at but hadn't actually read a word of. "Nothing, nothing. Yes, let me see the mock-ups," he said, trying to focus. The *Lusso* line was his signature design, something that he was proud of, perhaps the pinnacle of his established career, but even the joy of seeing his new shoe line come to fruition wasn't enough to overshadow the worry in his heart. His thoughts strayed and he exhaled a short breath as he confessed, "My mind is unruly today. Forgive me, my love. Perhaps I can look at these later."

"Of course, Enzo," she said, smiling. He leaned back in his chair and invited her to join him. She promptly settled on his lap, wrapping her arms around his neck. "Something is bothering you. Are you worried about the new line? If so, don't be. It's your most innovative design yet. People will be clamoring to own an Abelli Lusso."

He smiled briefly. If only that were his sole concern. At one time, his business had consumed his life—something he regretted now as it seemed he'd missed out on a lot with CoCo—but today, he was more concerned that the threats were getting more vicious and the most precious thing in his life wasn't shoes as it turned out. "These threats...they get more cruel, more taunting. What am I supposed to do?"

"You are doing everything in your power," Georgina said, not the least bit concerned. "This will blow over and then there will be nothing but people singing your praises for this new line."

Ordinarily, he enjoyed Georgina's flattery, but today it only served to irritate him. "Woman, this is serious. There is more at stake than just the latest shoe design to hit a bloated market," he said, encouraging her to leave his lap. She slid off with an uncertain expression and he softened. It wasn't Georgina he was upset with. "My apologies. I am in a terrible mood today. I am, perhaps, feeling my age." Georgina nodded but she still seemed wounded by his curt words. "Let me make it up to you... Perhaps something to brighten that beautiful neck?"

"You are too good to me," Georgina said, casting her gaze demurely before scooping up the plans and hugging them to her bountiful chest. "Please stop worrying. Everything will work out. You will see."

Ah, the blind confidence of youth. He wished he was comforted by her assurances. Unlike Georgina, who had nothing to lose, he had everything to lose. He kept their relationship private so it wasn't public knowledge that they were intimate. Not even CoCo knew of his intimacies with his assistant and he wished to keep it that way. Somehow, he knew his opinionated daughter would have something to say about that and he didn't wish to hear it. Georgina kept him young, which at his age, he valued more than he should.

He thought of CoCo's mother, Azalea, and for a moment lost himself to nostalgia. Perhaps one of his biggest regrets was letting her go. He'd been a brash, hotheaded idiot back then but by the time he'd figured out that he'd screwed up, Azalea had moved on. Burying himself in work had been his salvation. He should've worked harder to save his marriage. He should've been a more attentive father.

A single tear snaked down his cheek and he wiped it away in surprise. He wasn't prone to tears. It was the situation, pressing down on him. He couldn't seem to shake the feeling that something terrible was about to happen.

Hopefully, the FBI found this crazy person before his bad feeling turned into a self-fulfilling prophecy.

ONE DRINK SHOULDN'T be too bad, Rian told himself even though his nerves were drawn taut. That dress was doing terrible things to his resolve and he couldn't seem to keep his eyes where they belonged. Sweat popped along his brow and he wiped it away before the she-devil bewitching him saw it. That's all he needed, her knowing that she was doing a number on him. He'd never live it down. He wouldn't put it past her to prance around naked just to get his goat.

She sidled up to the bar and he followed after a quick look around the place to get situated. He always made sure he knew where all the exits were in case things went sour. True to her word, the place was small enough, not too crowded and didn't make him want to leave the second he stepped over the threshold.

"See? It's nice, isn't it?" she prompted him for his opinion and he grunted an answer. "I'll take that as a yes, though I'm not exactly fluent in caveman."

"Yes, it's fine," he said, looking to the bartender. "A beer, whatever's on tap."

"Beer? That's some sophisticated palate you have," she teased, then said, "How about this…I'll order for us both."

"I like beer," he said, not trusting her choices. "I don't like sweet, froufrou drinks."

"And you make the assumption that I do? Actually, I'm a whiskey girl. Jameson, actually." At his open look of surprise she smiled and said, "I got a taste for it when I was traveling abroad in Ireland. Don't tell my father, though. He'd fall over in a faint. He's a wine snob."

"I don't mind a shot of Jameson," he said, gesturing for her to go ahead. "But the deal was one drink."

"Well, that was the initial offer. How about a counteroffer?"

"Such as?" Why was he encouraging her? One drink was all that was sensible. Anything after that was dangerous. But he liked the way her eyes sparkled with mischief and, again, that dress was messing with his head so he humored her. "What's on the table? It'd better be good."

"How about this…we will play a game. We'll play I've Never. If you lose two out of three I've Nevers, you have to drink, but if you win, I drink."

"That's not a fair game. I know quite a bit about you, thanks to the tabloids. Plus, how are we supposed to know if either of us is lying?"

"I'll be completely honest." Her devilish smile was damn adorable. "Are you in?"

Well, hell, this was a bad idea, but he was intrigued. "One round," he said.

"Winner chooses if we play again."

He laughed. "Okay, prepare to lose, sweetheart."

"We'll see."

"Ladies first."

She wiggled on her bar stool, a happy smile curving her generous lips. "I've never…been in a threesome."

Her opener was a doozy and it packed a punch. Going straight to questions sexual in nature was like throwing gunpowder on a fire. He licked his lips and chuckled, the sound a little strained. "You sure you want to go there first?"

"Is it true or false?" she said and he stifled a groan. How'd that girl manage to make innocent look sexy as hell? "Clock is ticking."

"No one said anything about there being a time limit."

"Ten seconds."

She was a wild thing. At least, according to the tabloids. He took a chance. "False."

CoCo laughed and shook her head. "Sorry, haven't done that. What do you take me for?"

He laughed, not willing to touch that one with a ten-foot pole. "All right, you got me on that one. Next."

"I've never...shot a gun."

He didn't hesitate on this one. "True."

"Very good. I hate guns." Her expression turned playfully serious. "Okay, here it goes...answer this one right and I drink...answer wrong and it's down the hatch the whiskey goes for you."

"Hit me. I'm just getting warmed up now."

"So confident. Okay, I've never...been in love."

Oh, that was easy. He couldn't imagine anyone capturing this girl's heart. "True," he answered without a doubt but she shocked him when she shook her head.

"Sorry...false. I have been in love. Drink up, buddy."

"I don't believe you."

She met his gaze. "And why not?"

"Because you don't seem the type to fall for anyone. You're like one of those wild birds that would go stir-crazy in a cage."

She laughed but there was a slightly sad note to the sound as she said, "Well, you're wrong. I did fall in love a long time ago. Now drink up."

He wasn't a quitter or a cheater so he downed the shot as directed. He lost fair and square. But the game did stir more questions. Who was this guy who managed to steal CoCo's heart? He gestured for another round, then turned to CoCo. "Okay, so who was the guy?"

"Sorry, that's not part of the game," she said, grinning. "Your turn."

She wasn't going to spill that intel. He could respect that even if he was burning to know the details. Why? He didn't really know but he wanted a glimpse into the real CoCo, not the tabloid princess, and there was something burning in his chest that felt a lot like envy for the mystery guy who'd been given an all-access pass when everyone else had to stand outside. He cleared his throat and said, "I've never…committed a felony."

CoCo watched him from beneath a curtain of lush, dark lashes and then said, "True."

"Are you sure?"

"Hey, no fair trying to make me second-guess my decision."

He shrugged. "I didn't see that in the fine print."

A faint, playful scowl followed as she said, "Well, it's there. No pressuring or making me second-guess. And yes, my answer stands. You're not a bad boy, even if you try to come off as one."

"Is that so?"

"Yeah. Deep down, you're just a softie."

That made him laugh. "Really? That's how you see me? If I didn't know better, I'd say you're already drunk."

"Okay, so spill…true or false?"

He relented. "True." Her squeal of laughter lit up his insides and he was smiling before he could stop it. "But I came damn close once. That should count for something. If it weren't for my brother pulling some strings…yeah, I might've had a felony on my record."

"Ooooh, such an *almost* bad boy."

"All right, all right, Giggles. Here's your next one. I've never…worn women's underwear."

"Oh, that has to be true," she said.

"False!" At her surprise, he said, "It was on a dare in high school and they were the head cheerleader's bikini panties. And I rocked them, if I'm being honest."

"Okay, you got me there. Next question."

He thought long and hard. The whiskey shot was doing its job of loosening things up between them but he was having a bit too much fun. He grinned as he thought of his last statement. "I've never drank with a client."

"That's totally false."

He met her confident stare and he said, "Nope. Sorry, princess. This is my first time." And right about now, he had a good idea why he stood by that rule, because she was a heartbeat away from getting kissed.

HER HEART RACED and she leaned toward him, almost able to taste those luscious lips, but then Rian pulled back and the spell was broken. CoCo didn't bother hiding her disappointment but she didn't comment because she already knew what he was going to say and she didn't want to hear it. Instead she gestured for another round but he put the kibosh on it.

"We've had plenty. Rounds of whiskey are a recipe for bad decisions. It was a fun game, though."

She switched gears and slid from the bar stool. "Fine. I'm ready to go dancing now anyway."

"Dancing? I don't think so."

"Oh, I do think so. In fact, I insist. We can pop over to my favorite club, Tinsel, and meet up with some friends of mine."

"That's a double no," he said sternly. "A nightclub is a logistical nightmare."

"Stop being such a worrywart. Everything will be fine. How could anything happen with hundreds of people watching?" She tugged at his shirt. "C'mon, it'll be fun. I promise!" She ignored his protests and dragged him outside to hail a cab.

"What are you doing? We drove here."

"Safety first. We've been drinking. And if we take a cab, we can drink some more. I suspect there's a cool guy lurking beneath that suffocating layer of buzzkill you hide behind and I want to get to know that guy."

"Yeah, well, that guy isn't on the clock," he said, gracing her with a stern look that oddly made him ten times sexier. Maybe it was the whiskey talking but CoCo wouldn't mind sampling those lips or caressing that firm, set jaw. "We should get back to the hotel."

"If we return to the hotel right now, these clothes are coming off. However, if you let me get a little club time, I swear I will docilely return to the hotel and promise to keep my hands to myself and my clothes on. Sound like a deal?" She waited with bated breath, half hoping he'd drag her back to the hotel, but when he grudgingly agreed with a black look, she smiled, happy to enjoy a win either way. "Great. You'll love Tinsel. It's filled with hotties almost every night."

"I'll keep that in mind when I'm not being dragged there against my better judgment."

She laughed. "Such a sourpuss. Oh! Here comes a cab. Let's go," she said, moving quickly to the cab and climbing in before he came to his senses.

"This is a bad idea," he muttered, mostly to himself until CoCo swung her long legs over his and stretched them out. He jerked his gaze away and she giggled. The fact that he continually pretended that he wasn't affected by her charms was entertaining, even if it was a bit maddening. She wasn't accustomed to being so blatantly ignored, much less rejected. It was a new thing—and while the novelty was something, she suspected she wouldn't enjoy it becoming a trend.

"Why do you pretend that you're not attracted to

me?" she asked boldly. "I can tell when a man is interested. You're not fooling anyone."

"I don't mess around with clients."

Ah, the rules again. She'd never met a man so consumed with toeing the line. "What if I wasn't a client?"

Rian swallowed but he kept his voice firm. "I don't mess with party girls."

Her smile froze, her former good mood dimming a bit. "Is that what I am? A party girl?"

Rian swung his gaze to meet hers. "Seems like it to me."

"Perhaps I'm more than that and you just haven't chosen to see farther than your nose."

He graced her with a derisive look that stung a little. "Not likely, princess."

CoCo swung her legs off him and tugged at her dress. What did she care what Rian thought? His opinion meant little to her. Still, she couldn't keep the hurt from her voice as she said, "Well, I guess I'd better live up to that reputation."

"Hey, don't get hurt feelings now," he said. "Who says there's anything wrong with being a party girl? It's the way you live your life."

Was he trying to comfort her after basically calling her out? She didn't want his pity. *Screw this.* She needed a drink and a good time. She shrugged. "I'm fine. Just looking forward to getting out of this cab and having a cute bartender put a drink in my hand. Time to get this party started."

Rian looked primed to add something else but he held it back and she was glad. She didn't want to hear any more condescension from that chronically handsome mug. He had the ability to make her feel bad and want to make a good impression at the same time, which wasn't healthy. She didn't need him. He was a temporary inconvenience. After this gig, he would be gone and she'd gladly say goodbye.

The cab stopped in front of Tinsel and she bailed, almost leaving him behind. *Gotta be quick on your feet if you want to keep up with this party girl.* She graced a smile to the bouncer, who recognized her as a regular and let her past the rope, but when Rian tried to do the same, the bouncer gave him guff. She could've smoothed the way for him but a mean part of her wanted him to wait his happy ass outside while she found her friends.

"CoCo!"

She sent him a short smile over her shoulder and then disappeared into the club, leaving him behind.

9

GODDAMN HER. SHE'D purposefully left him behind. He shoved a few hundred-dollar bills into the bouncer's hand and then entered the club, percolating with irritation that CoCo had blatantly ditched him. Had that been her plan all along or had he pissed her off with his comment in the cab and this was her way of punishing him? He wasn't sure but he had a niggling sense that his comment had been the catalyst. She'd gone from playful and mischievous to cool and distant in a matter of seconds after he'd made his party-girl comment. He didn't understand why that had made her mad. For crying out loud, it'd been her idea to go out to a club, which clearly supported his statement.

He stalked into the throbbing din, immediately assaulted by the raucous noise that passed itself off as music, and wound his way through the writhing crowd. Yeah, this was a huge mistake. Already his intuition was clanging like a bell at how much of a security nightmare this place was. Multiple areas for someone to hide out and the dim lighting, coupled with the strobing, gave him an instant headache.

He kept his eyes peeled for CoCo and like a magnet his gaze was drawn straight to that smoking body in that impossibly tight dress. She was surrounded by guys, all trying to buy her a drink, and she was playing them like a bluegrass fiddler. It was almost entertaining to watch—except when one guy's hand crept too close to her ass for Rian's comfort and he had to smother the urge to permanently remove the guy's hand.

This was a game to her. She was playing him as easily as she played every guy, that was apparent. *So calm down, cowboy,* he told himself. Instead of rushing to extricate her from the crowd, he kept her in his line of sight and let her play her game without him. Finding an empty booth, he slid in, watching as CoCo laughed prettily and flirted with every single man trying to butter her up.

Suddenly, a slinky redhead joined him, her dress nearly as tight as CoCo's, except it appeared to be made from lace and was pretty much see-through. "Fancy seeing you here, handsome," she said with a perky grin. "You don't recognize me, do you?"

He tried hard to jog his memory but he was still trying to keep one eye on CoCo and failed. "Sorry. Remind me," he said with a brief smile.

"I'm Stella. I saw you at CoCo's party the other night. Did you two hook up?" she asked with casual interest and he couldn't stop the glower, but she didn't take offense. "I just figured you were her new boy toy or something. She's always got someone on the hook, you know?"

Yeah, that didn't surprise him. "It's not like that."

"Oh? Do tell. What is it like?"

"I'm just helping her family out right now."

Stella smiled at the intrigue and sidled closer, her drink in hand. "Then that means you're single and ready to mingle? That's the best news I've heard all night."

There was no doubt that Stella was stunning and ordinarily, Rian wouldn't cry in his beer if this hot number curled up on his lap, but he wasn't buying what she was selling. He wanted to say it was because he was working a job but there was a nagging sense that his reluctance went deeper than that. "You and CoCo are close?" he guessed.

Stella twined her fingers together and said in a sing-song voice, "Besties, baby." She offered a sip of her drink and after a moment's hesitation, he took it. She smiled and pushed it toward him. "You look thirsty. Go ahead."

He was thirsty and if he went to the bar, he'd lose his vantage point. He figured one drink wasn't going to put him over the edge. "Thanks," he said, swallowing the rest of what tasted like rum and Coke. Best friends, huh? Maybe she'd know more about who was targeting the Abelli family. "How long have you been close?"

Stella pretended to think, then said, "This conversation is boring. Let's dance." And then she grabbed him by the hand and pulled him onto the dance floor. He caught CoCo's gaze just as Stella looped her arms around his neck, pressing her lithe body against his, startling him with how boldly she ground against him. *Holy hell.* This woman was aggressive. And then she cupped his groin! He stiffened in shock. "That's some equipment you're working with," she purred. "I wouldn't mind taking you out for a spin." He was seconds away from extricating himself from the woman's grip when CoCo appeared, eyes blazing.

"I thought you were on the clock," she said, throwing his words back at him before glaring at Stella.

"What? You didn't call dibs," Stella said defensively. "And he was sitting all by himself, like a sad puppy. I felt obligated to show him a good time. I mean, look at him…he's a full-course meal. Maybe we can share?"

"Stella, stop embarrassing yourself. He's not available."

"Says who? I don't see a ring on his finger."

"Says me."

Was it terrible that he was mildly entertained by the fact that two hot women were bickering over him? Okay, his ego was entertained, but his brain told him to nip everything in the bud before things got out of hand. "All right, all right, it was just some harmless fun. Everyone back to your corners."

CoCo hit him with an openly cranky look. "Yeah, it looked harmless. Looked to me like you and Stella were about to hump each other's brains out right here on the dance floor."

"Oh, please. Like I would do that," Stella said, bored and irritated at the same time. "And what is your problem? Who shoved the mega-stick up your butt tonight? Prudey CoCo is no fun, whatsoever." Without waiting for a reply, Stella stalked off, leaving CoCo and Rian amid the dancing crowd.

"You wouldn't dance with me but you'll dance with her?" she asked, crossing her arms and glaring.

A grin found him and he didn't stop it even though he knew it would likely make things worse. "You seemed busy on your own." And then he reached out and pulled her abruptly into his arms, shocking her. Now, this was a whole new level of bad idea but it felt pretty good. "Is this better?" he asked.

Molded against him CoCo softened a little, and it did something to his insides that he didn't trust but craved more of. When Stella moved against him, it had felt dirty. But when CoCo did it…it felt like the most incredible thing in the world. His hands framed her hips as they moved together, the music entering his bloodstream like an aphrodisiac, winding around his senses and squeezing in a sensual way that immediately put him on alert.

"I don't feel right," he admitted, though everything was beginning to come alive in the most incredible way, from the feel of CoCo in his arms to the epic throb of the music. He growled as lust pounded in his veins and he pulled CoCo more tightly against him. "You're killing me."

She drew a sharp breath and lifted her lips, sealing her mouth to his, and he lost all sense of control.

This was all sorts of bad.

And he couldn't seem to care enough to stop.

A WILD THRILL raced through CoCo as Rian's tongue invaded her mouth in a possessive sweep that nearly knocked the strength out of her knees. Good God, he was a good kisser, she thought as he dominated her senses and held her as if the world were coming to an end and they were the last two people on earth. Everything about the moment was surreal and incredibly hot but there was also something vaguely disturbing about it, too. Rian wasn't acting like himself. Or was he? She wasn't sure. She couldn't quite tell. Usually he had a rigid sense of duty that clung to him but right now, he was an overcooked noodle, all loose and easy, which was a nice change but something didn't feel right. She gripped his face and stared into his eyes. "Are you feeling okay?"

"I can literally feel the music in my bones," he said with a sense of perplexed wonder. "I don't think that's normal. I don't even like this kind of music but right now, it's pretty amazing."

"Did Stella give you something?" she asked, straining to hear Rian amid the din of the music. His hips swiveled in time to the beat and she lost her train of thought for a moment. He had the sexiest moves! She couldn't help but imagine those hips thrusting against her, penetrating her with the cock that Stella had put her grubby hands on.

Focus, CoCo. If Stella had doped Rian, she'd kill the woman. "Rian, pay attention…did Stella give you something, like a pill?"

He shook his head but the faint troubled frown as he searched his memory gave her a bad feeling. "Her drink. She gave me her drink. Rum and Coke, I think. Why?"

Damn her. Stella had no doubt put Molly in the drink for herself but then, when she'd given Rian her drink, he'd gotten dosed instead. "Rian…I think you've been dosed with Molly," she said with a worried groan. This was all sorts of bad. "I'm sorry! I could kill her for this. We should take you back to the hotel before things get out of hand."

"What are you talking about?" he asked, rubbing at his eyes. "She drugged me?"

"How do you feel?"

"Weird. Like I want to…"

He didn't need to finish his sentence. She could see

it in his eyes and it took her breath away. A part of her wanted desperately to strip him bare and ride him as if there was no tomorrow but she knew that Rian wasn't thinking clearly and it wasn't right.

"We should go," CoCo said, using the last bit of will-power she had to do the right thing.

"The music…the lights…" he groaned as he pulled her back into his arms. "Incredible."

"It's the drug. It heightens your senses," she said, winding her fingers through his hair, unable to stop herself from moving with him, their bodies fitting to-gether like two puzzle pieces. It was too easy to imag-ine how well they'd fit without the barrier of clothes between them. The tantalizing scent of his body toyed with her good intentions and she lost herself to the sen-sual awareness buzzing between them. "You smell so good," she murmured, burying her nose against his chest, loving how strong and firm he felt.

"This is bad," he said with a tinge of panic that snapped her out of her sexual haze. He shook his head as if trying to clear his mind but she knew that wasn't going to help. The drug had to run its course. "I want to bury myself inside you," he said baldly, his gaze hot and bothered, his touch urgent.

God, yes! Please do it! The words bounced in her head, but she managed to keep them to herself. The last thing either of them needed was to throw gasoline on the raging fire that was already crackling. "Let's get you out of here," she said, grasping his hand and pull-ing him away from the dance floor.

She was racked with remorse for dragging him here against his will and she could kill Stella for dosing Rian like that. Not for the first time she wondered if

Stella was all that good of a friend but she had bigger concerns.

She motioned for a cab and one appeared within moments. After stuffing Rian into the back, she climbed in beside him. She had just enough time to give the cabbie the hotel address when Rian grabbed her and pulled her straight to his mouth and all restraint broke.

It was a free-for-all. Hands everywhere, mouths followed, legs twined together and lust surged. It was a dirty, desperate, you're-gonna-regret-this-in-the-morning kind of action and CoCo had never been so aroused by one man. If it were possible to get any hotter, she would've combusted in a fiery explosion of skin and bone.

And she really couldn't remember why Rian had resisted in the first place, because things were finally getting interesting.

10

HE COULDN'T GET enough of CoCo. The touch of her skin, the taste of her kiss. She was unlike anyone he'd ever been with and the clothes between them were an irritant that he couldn't stomach a moment longer. Stumbling into their hotel room, they were ripping each other's clothes off as he slammed the door shut with his foot. That tight dress was the first to go and suddenly there she was, standing in all her glory, naked as the day she was born, and Rian nearly fell to his knees to worship at the vision that was CoCo Abelli. This was why men sacrificed their souls to this woman. She was exquisite. And even though he'd gotten an eyeful earlier that day, it was nothing compared to feasting on every hill and curve as he dropped to his knees and drew her close, that delectable feminine vee beckoning him like a siren song.

Her hands went to his shoulders and he buried his face between her thighs, seeking and finding that sweet, pulsing core. She shuddered and his fingers squeezed her ass, invading her musky sweetness with his tongue until she was shaking and moaning, barely able to stand.

Everything was ten times more visceral and the primal feelings raging through his body made him feel like a caveman taking his woman.

CoCo stiffened and cried out, pushing against his shoulders, and he knew she'd come. Grinning with dark satisfaction, he rose and scooped her into his arms. "You taste incredible," he said, knowing he could eat her all day and never utter a word of complaint. He craved those little shudders and quakes, those tiny mewling pants and the way she gasped nonsensical strings of words as she climaxed. Oh, yeah, he could listen to that melody all day long. He kissed her long and deep, loving that she could taste herself on his tongue. Nothing was sexier.

"Rian," she gasped, still trying to catch her breath. "We have to stop. You don't want to do this…"

"Like hell I don't," he growled. He couldn't think straight. He had CoCo on his tongue and his cock was so hard it was nearly splitting in two. "You're the most amazingly beautiful woman I've ever seen." He pressed kisses to her neck, moving toward her breasts, dipping to suck those hard peaks into his mouth, twirling the nipple in his mouth until she writhed beneath him. Her groans pushed him to the point of delirium. Her skin was glazed with a thin sheen of sweat as her damp brow was evidence of her earlier orgasm. Her legs wrapped around his torso and her hot core pressed against his cock, contradicting her words telling him to stop. But there was something in his brain that registered the faint request and he pulled up short, his limbs shaking as he held himself back. "Princess, what's wrong?" he asked, his head swimming. "Did I hurt you?"

She shook her head and her hands shook as she

smoothed her hands over his chest, lingering on the sparse tufts of curly hair on his sternum. "You don't understand…it's the Molly…you're going to wake up tomorrow and hate yourself if we don't stop."

CoCo's words penetrated the haze and he knew she was right but he couldn't fathom stopping. He wanted her so bad he thought he'd die if he didn't plunge inside that tight heat but he couldn't trust that what he was feeling wasn't just because of what CoCo said.

He groaned and rolled off her to fall on the bed, covering his eyes. What was happening to him? His cock was a kickstand, lifting off the nest of groin hair, seeking what was being denied, and he thought he'd never survive the night like this. "What the hell was in that shit?" he asked, still reeling from the sexual high. "My skin feels like it's been turned inside out and every nerve ending is exposed."

"I don't know what Stella was tripping on so I can't say exactly what she gave you," CoCo answered, her breasts heaving as she tried to slow down. Her breasts were something he'd never experienced and he couldn't help but reach out and pinch a nipple. She gasped and jerked, her hips thrusting as she rubbed herself with a moan. "Don't make this worse. I want to do the right thing but you're making it impossible."

Rian rolled over and climbed on top of her, unable to stop kissing her. She didn't stop him. Their tongues tangled and twisted, plunging and tasting until they were so heated and turned on that there was no stopping what was coming.

He lifted and bent her legs, placing her feet against his shoulders, and then guided himself inside her with a nice, smooth glide, burying himself to the hilt into her wet heat. He nearly blacked out from the pleasure. Everything was tight and hot, squeezing him from all sides.

"Oh, my God," he breathed, his eyes rolling up into his head as he lost himself in the pleasure of sliding in and out of that wonderful sheath. She lifted her hips for a deeper thrust and he obliged, going as deep as he could. He caught her gaze, her lips parted, and he was struck by the connection—a soulful and meaningful connection that came out of nowhere—and he squeezed his eyes shut, needing to come before he lost his mind. But his orgasm kept dancing out of reach. Just as he thought he'd reach that pinnacle, he would lose the sensation and have to start over.

They switched positions and soon he was thrusting into her from behind but he couldn't pull the trigger. After an hour of trying and failing, Rian groaned and withdrew, falling to the bed with a pissed-off growl. "This ain't happening. I don't know what's wrong."

CoCo climbed on top and positioned herself on his cock. The view was spectacular but he wasn't sure it was going to happen. "It's the drug," she told him breathlessly. "It helps guys stay hard longer. I'm not complaining." A grin followed as she began to move against him. "Here, let me do some of the work."

Watching CoCo slowly grind on his cock was the most incredible thing he'd ever experienced. Gripping her hips, he feasted his gaze on that sweet feminine place that was the center of his universe at the moment and then, when CoCo lifted herself to swivel carefully, going reverse cowgirl, he lost it. After a few good pumps with that luscious ass facing him, her head thrown back with abandon, he came so hard his toes curled, crying out until he was hoarse with each cresting wave.

Shuddering seconds later, CoCo slumped forward for a brief moment before she could manage to slowly ease off his cock. She collapsed beside him, a happy, dazed smile on her face that did wondrous things to his ego. His mind was still spinning and his body hummed with postcoital satisfaction but he could sense the drug still messing with him because right now he just wanted to cuddle.

Cuddle?

"When does this drug wear off?" he asked, fighting the urge to tuck her into his side and fall into a blissful sleep. "I still don't feel right. My head's throwing all sorts of strange crap my way."

She giggled, sounding slightly drunk. "You just broke your Molly cherry. Is it true you never forget your first time?"

It wasn't funny—if he were thinking straight, he'd be pissed as hell—and yet he began to laugh, too. It made no sense. Neither did the fact that, in spite of knowing it was out of character, he reached for CoCo and pulled her tight into the cove of his body, nuzzling her neck and inhaling the unique, intoxicating scent that was all her own. She smelled like sex, woman and the wild thrill of something taboo, and he couldn't get enough. "You smell incredible," he groaned, feeling as if he would never be able to get enough.

"It's the Molly." She sighed happily. "Don't read too much into it."

Her honest answer should've reassured him that he wasn't losing his mind over a woman he'd been ready to pitch into a lake only hours earlier. There was something that rang a little false inside him but he couldn't trust his feelings on this. He was out of his mind. Everything was clear as mud. Tomorrow he'd deal with the fallout. Right now, he just wanted to sleep with CoCo in his arms.

At that moment, nothing seemed sweeter.

IT WAS A long time before sleep found CoCo. She'd had a chance to take a dose at the club but she'd turned it down. Ordinarily, she would've taken it without thought but Rian's words had been ringing in her head about how everyone wrote her off as a party girl and nothing more. She hated being so marginalized, even if it was her own fault. So she'd turned it down and then she'd noticed Stella grinding on Rian like a stripper on a pole and she'd seen red. Was it jealousy that made her crazy when he'd been willing to dance with Stella and not her? It should make some difference that Stella had dragged him out there but CoCo had hated seeing him pressed against Stella like that. She'd never been possessive in her life but Rian brought out all sorts of hidden traits. Like caring about her reputation. Wanting more out of her life. Stuff like that.

Her mind was moving at a clip, her thoughts bouncing from one thing to another, all while she was cradled in Rian's arms like something precious. He felt good pressed against her, his light snore telling her he was out like a light. His body was something that she would fantasize about for years to come. Screwing around with Rian hadn't been wise but when Molly was in charge, everything tactile was on the menu—and sex was the main course. Even though the sex had been fantastic, she felt wretched for Rian. He'd been dosed without his knowledge and taken on a ride that he hadn't signed up for. She'd straight up kill Stella for doing that to him. It wasn't funny and it wasn't okay. The fact that she hung out with someone who thought it was no big deal to dose a stranger made her feel dirty.

Although it felt as if she'd just shut her eyes, she awoke with Rian around 9:00 a.m. At first they were both disoriented but Rian quickly came to his senses and rolled away from her to stumble unevenly to the bathroom. He shut the door and CoCo rose blearily to squint at the bright light streaming into the cheap hotel room. Her mouth tasted as if a small animal had died in it and she reached for her bottle of water to chug it down. She listened for signs of life in the bathroom and when Rian emerged, there was no mistaking the cool distance in his expression.

Might as well get this over with. "I didn't know Stella—"

"Save it. I'm not really in the mood to talk about last night," he cut in, moving to grab his clothes and disappear back into the bathroom. She heard the shower going and she exhaled an unhappy breath, her head pounding. She guessed they weren't going to go for round two anytime soon.

Her body responded with delightful little aches and pains in private places, reminding her how vigorously they'd entertained each other last night, and she actually blushed when she realized she really wanted to feel him inside her again. He was a beast in bed. No shame there.

But judging by that dark look, touching her was the last thing he wanted to do anytime soon. He blamed her for what'd happened. As if she'd known that Stella had dosed him. Yeah, right. Stella was impossible to control, dosed or sober. But as she tried to formulate a reasonable explanation to that effect, she couldn't see how hanging out with a person like Stella was a good endorsement.

Her wounded pride began to take over and she started to lose that contrite feeling. Hadn't she tried to tell him that it was the drug causing him to be all over her? Was it really her fault that he couldn't keep his hands where they belonged? And furthermore, why was he drinking someone else's drink? Every idiot knew that you never shared drinks in a club. That was practically an *invitation* to get dosed.

She scooped up her discarded clothing and quickly dressed, starting to silently fume at his high-and-mighty attitude toward her. By the time he emerged, her temper was percolating at a fine clip and she was ready to give it to him.

"Look, don't you dare treat me like some dirty girl you picked up at the bar, banged and then can't get away from fast enough. I'm not that girl. And for the record I tried to stop you and you were all hands so you can quit with the holier-than-thou attitude because it's really pissing me off."

"Just drop it," he warned, his wet hair dripping onto his back as he threw his towel back into the bathroom. "I never should've gone to that stupid club with you. I ignored my gut instinct and look what happened."

"Exactly what happened? You got laid. I don't see any other guy crying in his beer when that happens. Get over yourself, Rian. It's just sex."

"Speaking from experience, no doubt," he quipped

and she flushed with rage. "Don't start fires you can't put out."

"I hate you, Rian Dalton," she said, her chest heaving from the exertion it took to keep from throwing anything within grabbing distance straight at his melon head. "You're a real dick."

"And you're a paparazzi's meal ticket. Now that we've established our previous roles...let's get back to the point of this relationship—obviously, things went south last night but it's not going to happen again. We're going to hole up for the next couple of days and pretend that what happened didn't actually happen at all. Got it?"

"Gladly."

"Great." He gestured to the shower and she shook her head, unable to believe his nerve. She didn't get discarded. If anyone got the boot, it was the guy, not CoCo Abelli. "Don't you want to shower?" he asked when she just stood there, rooted in impotent anger and the overwhelming desire to tackle him to the ground.

But she couldn't find the right words even as she seethed. She didn't want to admit it but she was hurt by his attitude, even though she shouldn't have been surprised. He'd been a jerk when they first met, and he was a jerk now. Leopards don't change their spots. She was stupid to believe anything different. *Screw you, Rian. Screw. You.*

"I need air." She barely managed the words before jerking open the hotel room door to step outside but as her foot cleared the threshold something exploded right by her face, showering her with slivers of shattered wood, and she screamed as Rian shoved her to the ground, covering her with his body. "What was that?"

she asked, fear congealing in her throat as bits of wood covered the ratty carpet.

"Stay here," he told her quietly as he slowly climbed to his feet, inching to the window, watching the open door intently. The sound of wheels squealing out of the parking lot followed and after shutting the door with his foot, he closed the curtains. He pulled her to her feet with a curt "Pack your stuff. We're leaving," and she couldn't control the shiver that ricocheted down her back.

"Was that…a bullet?" she asked, her lips numb. Had someone *shot* at her? *Are you kidding me?* She couldn't accept that, because if she did, that meant…her father was right and someone was truly out there trying to hurt her family.

"Whoever it was took off when they saw that they'd missed, but we're not sticking around to give them a second chance."

She nodded and tried to gather up her things with shaking fingers. Within moments, they were packed and ready to bolt out of there but she couldn't quite wrap her mind around the situation. "What if they're still out there? How'd they know where to find us? I thought you said this place was secure?"

"They must've followed us after the club and waited to make their move. They thought they were going to get a clean shot from the outside. They almost did. If whoever had been a better shot, your story would've had a different ending, which is why we're ditching this place and getting out of Dodge."

"And where exactly are we going? What if they're waiting to follow us again? Did you get a look at the car?"

"No, but they've split the area. It's broad daylight, and they missed their shot. They'd be idiots to stick around but we're not going to test that theory."

"But where are we going to go? They shot at me! They nearly took my face off!"

She was nearing hysteria. She could feel it bubbling under the surface of her shock. Funny how a near-death experience put things in perspective at the speed of light. But the fact that she'd nearly died was stealing her ability to remain calm.

Suddenly, Rian was at her side, gripping her arms firmly, his voice steady but urgent. "I won't let anything happen to you. I need you to trust me. Can you do that for me?" he asked. When she jerked a nod, he softened his voice and said, "Good. Now grab your bag. We're getting out of here." Then he groaned as he realized the Range Rover was still parked at the bar. "Guess we're cabbing it back to the bar," he said, irritated, and she nodded, too freaked out to remind him that driving hadn't been an option. Thankfully, within minutes a cab appeared and they left the hotel.

Once in the Range Rover, CoCo swallowed the lump of fear in her throat and looked to Rian, his jaw set and his gaze steady on the road. "Where are we going?" she asked, her mouth dry. "If we're not safe at one of your *safe* locations, where can we possibly go?"

"Someplace no one would think to look."

CoCo sent him a bewildered look. "Which is where?"

"The middle of nowhere, deep in the Kentucky back-woods."

"*What?* Did you say Kentucky?"

He met her gaze briefly to say, "We're going to

Woodsville, Kentucky. Trust me, no one is going to follow us there and even if they did…they'd never find where we're going."

11

RIAN MADE A quick phone call to Kane, left a voice message with short details and the fact that he'd changed his mind and then secured plane tickets for them. On the outside he was calm, switching into protector mode seamlessly, but on the inside he was berating himself for putting a client at risk.

Why'd he go to that stupid club? He never should've agreed to go. If it'd been anyone else, he would've easily shot the idea down without a second thought, but CoCo had twisted him into a pretzel and before he'd known it, he was caving. A pretty smile and a hot body were a dangerous combination on the right girl, he thought darkly. "We've got a two-o'clock flight. We need to hurry to make it. We'll rent a car when we land."

"Do we really need to go so far? I mean, *Kentucky?* That's so…rural."

Now that the shock was wearing off CoCo was second-guessing the decision to leave town, but that was too bad. If he had to hoist her over his shoulder and carry her onto the plane, he would do it. "Maybe we should tell the FBI agents handling the case that I've been shot at. I think they might need that information."

"After we land. We don't know who we can trust and I'm not taking any chances. I'll make the necessary phone calls after I've secured the new location. Until then, it's radio silence."

"But what about my dad?" she asked, worried. "He's going to freak out if I just disappear."

"I will contact your father. After we land," he repeated pointedly. "Do you not realize how close you came to eating a bullet, princess?" She flushed and nodded with a small, scared movement. "Okay, then you know this is serious. No more playing by your rules. We're playing by mine."

Her body shook with a delicate shiver and he had to look away. That tiny motion was too reminiscent of how she'd shook with pleasure last night each time his tongue had danced on her skin, lapping at her pretty pink nipples. He cut his thoughts off, jerking at the unruly direction of his mind. Lusting after her had put them in this position and it wouldn't happen again. "Look, I know it was scary but we'll get through this. I just need you to buckle down and listen for once in your life, because now, it matters."

"I just can't believe it. I mean, who would want to kill me? I've never hurt anyone."

"It's likely not about you," he answered. "Whoever is after your dad is looking for the easiest target. They know that you're the one who means the most to him and if they hurt you, they'll reach his Achilles' heel."

"But I don't know why anyone would want to hurt my father. He's a sweet old man who designs shoes, for crying out loud. I mean, you've met my father. Does he seem the type to create enemies?"

"You said it yourself, people with more are envied by those with less. And I hate to point out that your dad is more than just a shoe designer. He wouldn't have risen to the top without some cutthroat business skills to match those creative talents." She scowled at his logic but he couldn't sugarcoat it for her sake. "I know it's hard to imagine that your dad isn't the sweet old guy with everyone he deals with but I've found that people with extreme wealth have the persona they share with their close family and the persona they cultivate with business associates...and they are rarely the same."

"Well, my dad isn't living two lives," she said. "You're off base. My father is a good man."

"I hope he is. I hope that what you see is what you get but you have to be prepared if this investigation into who's threatening him reveals something unsavory about your dad."

"Like what?" she asked coolly.

Rian shrugged. "Too many variables to speculate. I'm just saying, be prepared."

"That's ridiculous. My father doesn't have skeletons dancing in his closet. Someone is going after him because they're jealous. Jealousy is an ugly emotion and can compel people to do crazy things."

"Agreed, but revenge motivates people, too."

She looked away. "I don't want to talk about this anymore. My dad isn't a bad man and I won't entertain the idea that he might be. End of story."

He didn't argue. He hoped she was right. In his experience, everyone had skeletons. He just prayed, for CoCo's sake, that whatever was creating this mess wasn't so big that it destroyed CoCo's faith in the one man she seemed to love unconditionally. He might be a dick but he wasn't that big of one. "You're probably right," he conceded for the sake of making peace. "But in the meantime, let's just focus on keeping you safe. We'll let the feds figure out the rest."

She nodded and decided to let it go.

Within the hour, they were boarded and headed to Kentucky…the last place he imagined he might go to find sanctuary.

THE PLANE RIDE was long but nothing compared to an international flight, and within a few hours they were in Kentucky, tucked away in a rental Ford F-150 and headed to some place called Woodsville. She was still in a daze, struggling with the knowledge that she'd come close to dying and that someone actually wanted to hurt her. It'd been so much easier to believe that her father had been overreacting than believing the threats were real.

Once out of the city the countryside was pretty enough, but she wasn't in the mood to appreciate the scenic splendor of rural Kentucky. In fact, tears were hovering too close to the surface for comfort and she didn't know if it was the fear of being watched or the fact that she was coming down from a drug that squeezed all the serotonin from her brain and left her with nothing but depression after the high. To say it could go either way was depressing in itself.

"You were pretty quiet during the flight. You okay?" he asked.

What a question. Was she okay? How was she supposed to respond to that? Of course she wasn't okay.

She'd been shot at. Who bounces back from an experience like that as if nothing had happened? But she didn't want to say any of that. "I'm fine," she lied. "Just tired." That part was true. She felt wrung out and her body was protesting the long plane ride after their epic sex session but she definitely didn't want to bring attention to that, either. "How much farther before we get to this place? I feel like we've fallen off the map."

"Good. That's exactly what we want anyone who happens to get a notion to follow to feel. Woodsville is about an hour still. If you want to sleep, go ahead."

She nodded and leaned against the door, using the seat belt strap to support her head. She closed her eyes and tried to sleep but she was too strung out to allow true sleep to come. She made an exasperated noise and sat up. "Sleep's not going to happen," she said, beginning to get cranky. "Tell me about this place. Where are we going and why?"

He sighed, resting his arm against the window frame. "Well, I grew up in Woodsville. It's a small town, no stoplights, a general store, a sprinkling of other stores, a school and a tiny hospital. That's about it."

"Yikes. Sounds like a prison."

He laughed. "Yeah, that's how I felt when I was growing up, but I had a shitty childhood so that might've influenced my opinion."

"You mentioned your father was a jerk."

"That's the understatement of the year. He was an abusive asshole. He didn't give two shits about his sons and when he was sober enough to realize he had two kids, he spent that time beating them. Well, he beat us when he was drunk, too, but it was easier to get away from him when he was three sheets to the wind."

CoCo didn't know what to say. How horrific for Rian. "So…are you and your dad…?"

"He's dead. Thank God. Heart attack. Couldn't have happened to a more deserving person, that's all I can say."

"Wow. I'm sorry."

"No need for that. It was a long time ago."

"Yeah, but that's still awful to have those memories, I would imagine."

"I don't think about the past. Can't do nothing about it so why bother letting it ruin your present?"

"Very philosophical."

"Nope. Just common sense."

She nodded, thinking. "So I imagine that Woodsville doesn't have many good memories for you?"

"Not many," he confirmed but added, "except for the Bradfords. They took me and my brother in on the pretense of offering us summer jobs and then they sort of adopted us, unofficially. Cora and Warren Bradford were about the nicest, kindest people God put on this earth and they saved our lives."

CoCo sat stunned by the private revelation and didn't know how to react. Rian made more sense now that she knew a little bit more about him. "So that's where we're going?" she supposed and he nodded. "I can't wait to meet the Bradfords," she murmured.

"Well, you'll get to meet Warren but sweet ol' Cora died last year. Cancer. Let me tell you, the world lost an angel the day she died. She was good folk. Never had kids of her own but she adopted scores of them throughout the years. Best sweet potato pie you've ever tasted, too."

"Sweet potato pie? I've never had it. What's it taste like?"

"Sort of like pumpkin pie but better."

"I like pumpkin pie," she said. "But then, how do you go wrong with any pie?"

"Exactly." He flashed her a brief grin and her stomach tightened. He returned his gaze to the road. "Anyway, Cora taught Laci a lot of her recipes so at least that legacy is continuing on."

"Who is Laci?"

"Oh, Laci McCall…"

"You mean the country superstar? The one who recently won a Grammy for her hit single 'Someday You'll Belong To Me'?"

"The very same. That song was about my brother, Kane, by the way."

"Wow. That's impressive," she said, forgetting about her aches and pains and general crankiness. "How'd they meet?"

"Nothing too glamorous. We all met as kids. Laci's dad was a bit of a rambler so he left Laci with the Bradfords each summer when he went logging to make money for the winter. Laci and Kane started a thing and it never went away, even when Kane joined the military and Laci went on to become a big star. They recently found each other again and, well, you know how the story goes."

"That's so romantic."

He laughed. "I guess it sounds romantic but they were spitting mad at each other for a long time. Couldn't hardly be in the same room together without World War III happening."

"That's passion. In Italy, a passionate woman is

something to treasure," she told him. "Passion is what keeps love alive. That spark."

"It also causes people to react emotionally. How do you think stalkers are born?"

"This is not the same," she disagreed. "Don't you believe in love? How can you share that incredible story about your brother and Laci McCall and not believe in love?"

"I didn't say I don't believe in it. Clearly, my brother hit the jackpot with Laci but I'm not so delusional that I think that it happens that way for everyone and frankly, I'm too busy with my life to chase after what could turn out to be a pipe dream."

She frowned. "That's so…depressing."

"Why?"

CoCo shrugged. "It just is. Love is what makes life worth living, otherwise you're just going through the motions until the day you die."

"Now, *that's* depressing."

"We die alone. Why should you be alone while you're living?"

He chuckled. "True. But I guess it's just not for me. I like having variety and being able to do what I want, when I want to. Can't do that if you're tied down."

His answers were honest. She shouldn't care how Rian felt about relationships or matters of the heart but there was a tiny part of her that cared a lot. It was that tiny part that bothered her. She wasn't the kind of girl who slept with a guy and suddenly went all gooey over him. In fact, most times it was the other way around. She couldn't count the number of times she'd been hounded by ex-lovers begging her to come back to them. She couldn't get away fast enough from those ones. So to feel that pinch when Rian admitted his personal philosophy was just par for the course. Shot at, on the run and now secretly pining for a man who wasn't the least bit interested…yeah, that's perfect.

12

THEY PULLED INTO the Bradford Ranch around six that night and even though he wasn't a fan of Woodsville, he loved the ranch. He inhaled a deep breath of the cleansing country air, taking in the faint scent of horses in the barn and cattle in the field, and something inside his chest loosened.

"This is gorgeous," CoCo admitted, taking in the huge rolling hills and the pretty, lazy creek carving its way through the green valleys. The setting sun bathed the hills in red and orange, setting a halo of light behind CoCo's head, and Rian had to look away before she realized he was staring too hard. Even hungover with dark circles under her eyes, hair in a tangle, she was breathtaking. It didn't help that he remembered with excruciating detail how luscious that body was beneath her jean shorts and top. "How many acres?" she asked.

"More than four hundred," he answered, grabbing their luggage from the bed of the truck. "It's a nice spread. Big enough to give enough space and small enough to manage."

"Four hundred acres is not small by any stretch of

the imagination," she corrected him with a small smile. "And the air is so clean. Reminds me of my dad's country home in Italy. So pretty and peaceful."

"Yep. Well, until you meet Warren's fossil of a dog, Dundee. I don't even know how he's still alive. Watch out if he stakes a claim at your feet. That dog has gas that could kill an elephant."

She laughed. "Thanks for the warning. Does your brother know we're coming?"

"He will once he listens to his voice mail. He and Laci are in Montana for a few weeks and the cell service is spotty. But he already offered up his place so we're good." He pointed at the beautiful farmhouse-style home to the left of the main house and said, "That's where we'll be staying. Laci got it in her head to build a replica of the original farmhouse and so, here you go. Nostalgia and modern convenience married up and created a five-star experience. I think you'll like it."

"It's amazing," she agreed as they walked toward the house. "And you're sure they won't mind?"

"It's fine." He plucked the spare key from under the pump where Kane told him it would be and handed it to her. "You go ahead and get situated. I'm going to let Warren know we're here so he doesn't come shooting in the dark when he hears us moving around outside."

She couldn't tell if he was serious or not and, given the fact that she'd just been shot at, he realized too late that joke was probably too soon, but she lifted her chin and trudged forward like a trouper and a spurt of pride followed. She was a tough cookie. He liked that about her. Hell, if he were being honest, he was starting to like a lot of things about her. Was he on a mission to totally screw up his life? If he kept up with thoughts like that, it would seem so. He headed for the main house and after a quick knock, he entered, immediately assaulted by the smells from the pleasant part of his childhood. Cora had always filled her house with the scent of baking. To this day he couldn't walk past a bakery without thinking of her and how she'd fattened him and Kane up as if it were her God-given duty to save them from starvation. Maybe it had been. He walked into the house through the kitchen and found Cora's dearest friend and bridge buddy, Adeline, cleaning up, a warm smile wreathing her plump face when she saw him.

"Well, look at who's here, Warren. You come here and give me some sugar," she instructed him with a happy grin. Adeline and Warren had gotten closer after Cora passed and it was a relationship that everyone supported because Adeline, who was a lot like Cora, was a perfect fit for Warren. "Why didn't you call? I could've whipped up something nice."

"Don't go to any trouble, Adeline," he said, wrapping the old gal in a hug. "Just here for a few days. How are you?"

"Can't complain. The Lord is good to us, for certain. Warren had a bit of a stomach bug last week but he's right as rain now." Right on cue, Warren entered the kitchen with a frown but otherwise looked as he always did.

"Woman, don't go sharing details like that. No one needs to know about my stomach bug," he groused but Adeline, much like Cora, never took offense at his gruff style and simply waved a dish towel at him with a wink. Warren, still hale and hearty in spite of his age, clasped Rian's hand in a firm handshake just as he'd taught both Dalton boys. A man had only one chance to make a first impression, he'd told them, and that started with a firm, manly handshake. No one liked a limp hand-shake. Couldn't trust a man who shook like that. Sur-prisingly, Rian had discovered that advice was pretty spot-on. "You look good, son. What brings you home?"

Home. A warm feeling filled his gut and he smiled. It felt good to be loved by this man. If only life had seen fit to give the Dalton boys to the Bradfords from the start. Imagine how their lives would've turned out different. Not that he was complaining, but he'd lied to CoCo. Sometimes he thought of the past and the bad memories always knocked the wind from his lungs. "You look pretty good yourself. I see Adeline is keep-ing you healthy with her Southern cooking."

"You flatter me," Adeline tittered but was already bustling around fixing him a plate of fried chicken left over from their supper. "You hungry?"

"I could eat," he said, grinning. "But would it be too much trouble to fix up two plates?"

That stopped Adeline. "Two? Did you bring a friend? Do you have a lady out there?" The hope in her voice was too much and he laughed.

"Sort of. I mean, yes. But she's a client. We're holing up here for a few days to get off the grid. Is that okay?"

"Of course it is," Warren said. "You never have to ask."

"Thank you, sir. I appreciate that. We'll stay out of your hair, I promise. In the meantime, I can help out with the chores if you like."

"I never turn away good help," Warren said, grin-ning. "Now eat up and get settled and we can chat in the morning. You good with a 5:00 a.m. wake-up?"

"I love that nothing ever changes around here," Rian said, though he was groaning privately at such an early wake-up. That was the one thing about ranch life that he didn't quite miss. Although a Kentucky sunrise was something to see. At least there was that. "See you bright and early."

"Good to have you, son," Warren said with genuine affection and then, after snagging a fresh cookie, returned to the living room, to read the paper, no doubt.

Rian turned to Adeline, who had already fixed up two plates and said, "Now, don't think that you're going to get away with not bringing that young lady over here to meet us. I don't care if she's a client or a lady friend, that's just Southern hospitality and you know it."

"Yes, ma'am."

"Dinner tomorrow night?"

There was no point in refusing. "Of course. Should we bring anything?"

"Just yourselves." Adeline's sunny smile was as sweet as Cora's pies ever were. Seeing Adeline made him miss Cora all the more. She caught his momentary falter and her expression softened. "Everything okay?"

"I was just thinking of Cora. Still miss her."

"We all do, honey. We all do. You can't know a woman like Cora and not feel the cold when she's gone, that's a fact."

He loved that Adeline understood and didn't feel threatened by their love for Cora. He'd always believed that God broke the mold after He'd made Cora but then he realized shortly after Cora's funeral that He'd actually made a spare with Adeline. He hefted the stacked plates covered in tin foil in his hand. "Thanks for this. I'm starved and this is going to hit the spot."

"Oh, go on with you. It's just fried chicken and some mashed potatoes. It'll stick to your ribs good, though."

He leaned over and kissed Adeline's cheek. "Perfect for a country boy like me," he said with a grin and she giggled with pleasure. Yep, so much like Cora it made his heart happy and sad at the same time. "See you tomorrow."

Adeline waved and returned to cleaning up the kitchen while Rian walked the short distance to Kane and Laci's house. He found CoCo thumbing through a photo album from Kane and Laci's wedding. "I got some food, courtesy of Adeline and Warren. Don't worry, you'll meet them tomorrow over supper." He set the plates on the table and walked over to CoCo to peer over her shoulder at the pictures. There was a picture of Rian and Kane, linked arm in arm, dressed in their tuxedos, grinning for the camera with plump cigars in their mouths. "Good times," he noted with a grin. "Hungry?"

She closed the album. "Starved. What do you have?"

He pulled the tin foil away from the plates. "Good old-fashioned, stick-to-your-ribs country cooking. It's made with butter, cream and all sorts of things that will make most LA girls run away for fear of putting on a pound or two, but it's going to taste like heaven in your mouth."

"Well, lucky for you, I'm only half LA girl and the other half is pure Italian, and my Italian side likes to eat." She took a seat and pulled her plate toward her for an exploratory sniff, then groaned. "Smells amazing. Fork?"

He found two forks and handed one to her, took a seat opposite her and tucked into his own plate. "Oh, yeah, that's the stuff. There's nothing like Southern cooking.

I've traveled the world but there's no place that can do comfort food like our Southern gals."

"It's pretty good," CoCo agreed around a mouthful. "Damn, those LA girls don't know what they're missing."

He laughed, enjoying the fact that CoCo wasn't throwing a fit over a plate of fattening food. He loved the way she made no apologies for digging in as a man would. He rather liked the Italian side of her. What did she call it? Passionate. Italian women were passionate. He liked it. He liked it a lot.

13

BARTO TRIED TO QUELL the rage that immediately spurted when he received the news. "How could you miss? You're supposed to be the best. Someone overinflated their talents, I see."

"She moved slightly to the left. I would've hit the target if she hadn't shifted."

"Not really interested in excuses, only results."

"Look, what do you want to kill her for?"

Barto folded his hands in his lap, smothering his urge to kill the incompetent man questioning him, but seeing as his funds were running low and he had no choice but to continue to use the man's services, he chose to smile instead. "Reasons," he answered. "Tell me how you're going to rectify your mistake and I'll forgive your serious lack of accomplishment."

The man, known only by his handle, Trigger, shifted on the balls of his feet, glowering. "Look, I had to split the scene. I took a risk during the day and it didn't pan out. It happens. I went back to the chick's place and she wasn't there. I don't know who she's with but he seems to have some skills. Her old man must've hired him to protect her."

"Good. I want him to know that everything he holds dear is at risk."

"Yeah, sure, but to go after his kid? Seems harsh. She seems like your average rich bitch from LA."

"She's the heir to his legacy and his only child. I want him to feel the agony of loss."

"Yeah, but she's, you know, innocent."

He cast an icy stare Trigger's way. "She has Enzo's blood in her veins. She was born tainted."

Trigger shook his head as if Barto was the one who was messed up and said, "Whatever, man. So what do you want me to do? They've split town. I don't have the resources to go follow this chick wherever she decides to go. Besides, you never said I'd have to deal with a bodyguard. This is going to double my fee."

Barto's blood pressure swelled. The man was going to nickel and dime him into the poor house. "You were adequately paid for the job that hasn't been completed. You will find a solution to this problem of your own making and you won't receive another dime. Am I clear?"

"And what if I tell you to screw yourself?"

Then I will drop your body into a lake and never think of you again. "I have resources. Pray I don't need to use them to dispose of you."

"Bullshit. If you had so many resources, you wouldn't have hired me to do your dirty work," Trigger scoffed and Barto knew that Trigger was no longer useful to him, that he was quickly becoming a liability. He pulled a gun with a silencer screwed to the end and without hesitation shot Trigger in the head. He didn't have time to waste on people who were of no use. His time was precious. Enzo Abelli took everything from his family and he would see to it that he paid, one way or another. He owed it to his papa, Vincent. "For you, Papa, I will see that Abelli scum wiped from the earth for what he did to you. I promise."

He rose and stepped over Trigger's body, careful to avoid the blood seeping into the dingy carpet. It would be days before his body was found, which would give Barto more than a good head start. He stopped and sneered at Trigger's face, frozen in shock. "Your name is stupid. *Trigger.*" He shook his head in disgust and closed the door carefully behind him.

CoCo AWOKE THE following morning, groggy and disoriented as she blinked at the delicate floral wallpaper climbing the walls and the bright white eyelet duvet she was tucked under. The shabby-chic decor was charming and comforting at the same time but for a brief moment she had no freaking clue where she was, until the recollection of being shot at less than twenty-four hours ago jogged her memory.

"Oh, that's right," she grumbled to herself and pushed the blanket off to rise from the soft bed. She yawned and stretched, going to the window, and immediately spied Rian, wearing a tight white tee and jeans, looking incredibly sexy in the early-morning light, striding across the yard with that fossil of a dog, Dundee, loping at his side. *Oh, damn.* That man was sin incarnate. Just looking at him made her want to throw him down and have her wicked way with him, but she didn't see that happening, since he was still sore at her for inadvertently getting him drugged, as evidenced by the fact that he'd chosen a separate room from hers.

Okay, so she felt a twinge of guilt about the drugging incident but she couldn't control the actions of her friends any more than she could control the tide.

She moved away from the window and wandered the room, taking in the sweet country flavor of the decor, and wondered what'd it be like to live in a place like this, removed from the world, tucked away in a tiny town where everyone knew everyone else's business. She smothered a small laugh. Actually, it kinda sounded like Hollywood.

She showered and went downstairs to see if coffee was on the menu and smiled with relief when she saw a small pot ready for her. There was also a plate of scones. "I love this place," she murmured as she selected a raspberry scone along with her coffee and wandered outside to have a seat in one of the dual rocking chairs on the porch. She imagined this was where Kane and Laci spent their mornings, two lovebirds, enjoying their country bliss. A pang of envy followed as she bit into her scone. *Oh, man, that's good.*

Rian walked into view and he climbed up the steps to join her, sliding into the other rocking chair with a grunt.

"I see you found the scones. Courtesy of Adeline. She's a baker, like Cora was. Prepare to be force-fed at any given moment."

"I don't mind," she said around a bite. "Where've you been? You're all sweaty and it's only eight in the morning."

"The Bradford Ranch is a working ranch, which means there's always work to be done. I was helping

Warren this morning with the cattle and then there was a section of fence that needed repairing so I was doing that."

"You know how to mend a fence?" she asked, impressed. "So handy."

"I know how to do a lot of things. Warren taught us as teenagers. We were eager to learn whatever he could teach us because we knew in order to get out of our dad's house, we needed skills that went above and beyond ducking a blow."

She swallowed, hating that Rian had such a terrible childhood. "Can I do anything? I feel bad just sitting around, eating scones."

"Do you know how to ride a horse?"

She nodded. "Of course. I've owned several."

"Excellent. Then you can come along with me when I go to check the southern gate. Warren has a hard time getting to it because the terrain is a little too rough for him. I told him I'd check it out."

"Sure. When?"

"Probably around eleven. If you ask nice, Adeline will pack us a lunch."

"Like a picnic?"

"Well, I guess. You want to eat, right?"

So much for that wild hope of a romantic gesture. "Yeah, of course."

"Great. I'll let you handle the food detail, then." He pushed himself out of the rocking chair with a slight wince. "Good God, anytime I think I'm in pretty good shape all it takes is one day on the ranch to remind myself that I'm such a city boy now."

CoCo smiled and watched him leave, enjoying the view of that luscious backside very much. She didn't know what he was talking about. He was the hottest country boy she'd ever seen. And even if he didn't think of a picnic as romantic in any way, she was about to change his mind.

Was it bad that she wanted a second chance with her bodyguard?

Maybe. But she was too selfish to care and she didn't mind admitting that, either.

Some opportunities were just too good to pass up.

RIAN WAS GRATEFUL to have the Bradford Ranch to hole up at but he was a mess of unanswered questions and raging guilt. While CoCo went to introduce herself to Adeline and in the process help pack a picnic for the afternoon, he made a call to Kane and hoped his brother was within cell range.

He was in luck because Kane picked up, though the line was scratchy. "Sorry, we're up in God's country and apparently God has no need for good cell service," Kane said. "I got your message, though. What the hell is going on?"

"I don't know how they found us. I used that old hotel on Juniper Street, off Exit 204. It's hardly ever used, no traffic, and it was dead when we checked in. But who-ever took a shot at CoCo had been waiting for us. The only thing I can figure, and it makes me sick to admit this but…they might've followed us back from the club."

"The club? I'm not familiar with that protocol," Kane said, being deliberately obtuse. "Because I know you didn't just admit to going out clubbing with a client, right?"

"Okay, you can bust my balls later. Right now, I need advice."

"I think busting your balls now is appropriate. What were you thinking? This isn't like you to be so unprofessional."

Rian gritted his teeth, hating getting dressed down by his older brother, but he knew he deserved it and Kane didn't even know all the details. He wavered on keeping the full details to himself but figured, seeing as Kane was his partner, as well as his brother, he'd better come clean. "There's more," he admitted with a heavy sigh. "I got drugged at the club and...things got heated between me and the client."

"What does heated mean?"

"We... Aw, hell, you gonna make me spell it out for you?"

"No, I get the message loud and clear. Man, what's gotten into you? Are you okay? Not still impaired, right?"

"I'm fine. Been working since 5:00 a.m. with Warren. Nothing like good old-fashioned backbreaking work to make you sweat out the toxins, you know?"

"Yeah, true enough. All right, so this isn't so bad that it can't be fixed. The client understands that it was just because of the drug, right? That you're not really into her like that."

"Yeah, sure," he lied. "It was the drug."

"Great. So, as long as you stay away from any narcotics for the rest of the gig, you should be fine."

"That shouldn't be a problem. I doubt Warren has any club drugs lying around."

"Yeah, Warren in a dance club, can you imagine?" Kane barked with amusement. "He'd have all those whippersnappers pulled out by their ears and put to work."

"Maybe that's what the world needs. More people like Warren," Rian grumbled, thinking of all the rich, useless young adults frittering away their youth with drugs and meaningless sex. Speaking of sex…a sudden memory of that intense connection between him and CoCo flashed in his mind and he tried to shy away from it. It'd been the drug. Logically, he understood that a chemical had been manipulating the pleasure centers of his brain but he was left with the residual yearning to touch CoCo again. That's why he'd deliberately put her in a separate room. He simply didn't trust himself to keep his hands off her body.

"All right, so you're safe for now. Did you call the FBI agents handling the investigation? They're going to want to know what happened."

"I will as soon as I'm done with you."

"Good. No one is going to find you at the Bradford Ranch so just hunker down and let the feds do the dirty work. In the meantime, enjoy some home cooking, help Warren around the ranch and, for God's sake, keep your damn hands off the client. There's more at stake than your libido."

"You don't have to lecture me on that," he told Kane. "I was on a drug, not trolling for chicks."

"I know, but I know a little bit about those so-called 'love drugs.'" When Kane didn't elaborate, Rian was left to wonder. "The thing is, they can't make you want someone you don't already have a passing interest in. If there'd been nothing there to catch fire, it wouldn't have happened, so be careful. You're attracted to a client and that's just bad news for our business. We don't mess with clients. Plain and simple."

"I know. I'm not going to touch her again. Lay off and stop lecturing me."

"Hey, don't get pissy. I'm just saying…time…sorry…casual…no good—" And then the line went dead. Perfect timing. Rian might've missed most of what Kane was trying to say but he could glean the gist of it and it was nothing he didn't already know.

He immediately called the agent in charge of the Abelli case. "This is Rian Dalton. There's been a situation. Someone took a shot at CoCo yesterday and in order to guarantee her safety, I've had to move her. We are at a secure location."

"You should've gained authorization before moving Miss Abelli. What's your location now?"

"Pardon me, agent, but I'm not working for you. I work for Mr. Abelli. If he wants to know where his daughter is, he can call me and I'll let him know. Other than him, no one else is going to know."

"Did you get a description of the shooter?"

"No. I heard tires squealing from the parking lot but I didn't catch the make and model. I was too busy making sure CoCo was all right."

"No injuries?"

"None."

"Is this a good number for contact later?"

"Yes. I'll keep my cell with me at all times."

"Good. We're getting close to finding the person responsible. We just need a few more days. We'll be in touch."

"Great."

He clicked off and tucked his phone in his pocket. A few days shouldn't be too hard. Beautiful country, plenty of work to keep him busy and the best food in the South.

Everything sounded perfect…except for the part where he had to keep his hands off CoCo. That part made him break out in a sweat.

He could do this. No problem, right?

14

CoCo knocked on the screen door leading into the kitchen and a plump woman with a shock of wavy white hair appeared at the door. "You must be Rian's friend, come in, come in," Adeline said, ushering CoCo into the kitchen. Immediately, CoCo was assaulted by the most heavenly smell and her mouth actually watered.

"Smells incredible in here," she said, glancing around looking for the source. "Rian said you enjoyed baking. If whatever you're making is as good as those scones, you've made a friend for life." She held her hand out with a smile. "I'm CoCo Abelli. So nice to meet you."

The older woman wiped her hands on her faded Thomas Kinkade printed apron and a bright smile wreathed her face. "What a beautiful name. CoCo Abelli, it really rolls off the tongue like an exotic dessert. I'm Adeline Verley, pleased to meet you, sugar. And to answer your question, I'm making fresh applesauce. I don't care for that store-bought stuff. You never know what they're putting in there and with all the reports about everything giving you cancer, you can't be too careful. The truth is, my dear friend Cora, God rest her soul, died from cancer and if I can do something to make a difference in someone's life, which means whipping up a batch of homemade applesauce for Warren because he loves it so much, I'll do it in a heartbeat." She winked. "And it makes the kitchen smell so yummy, doesn't it?"

"Very," she agreed. "So you and Mr. Bradford…"

Adeline waved away CoCo's unsure question, saying, "Oh, honey, if Rian thinks enough of you to bring you here, then I insist that we not stand on ceremony. Warren wouldn't hear of it. And yes, Warren and I are going steady, if you can call it that anymore." She bent to whisper conspiratorially, "Actually, we're plain living in sin but at our age, I figure we better take what we can get while the getting is good, right?"

CoCo laughed at the older woman's delightful candor and realized she already liked Adeline immensely. In fact, she reminded her of Miss Plix, her most beloved nanny, always ready with a smile to lend a hand to whoever needed it. Sadly, Miss Plix had died when CoCo was twelve from an undiagnosed heart condition. The one saving grace was that Miss Plix had died in her sleep. "I think it's wonderful that you're grabbing on to happiness wherever you can. Life moves pretty quickly, right?"

"Darn right it does. Now, what can I do for you?"

"Well, Rian sent me to find lunch fixings. He said you might be able to help me put something together. We're going to ride out and check the south gate for Warren. Rian said it'd be a good idea to bring along lunch. Is that okay?"

"Oh, honey, that's fine by me. Better than fine, actually. I worry when Warren takes it on himself to go to the far edges of the property. He hates cell phones and refuses to carry one so I never know if he's going to be all right. At our age, we can't be too careful but the old coot acts as if he's still sixteen."

Even though she was chastising his stubborn nature, the words were said with such warmth and open adoration that CoCo smiled. How lucky for Warren that he'd found a woman who seemed equally as wonderful as the first love of his life. "We're happy to help. Is there anything else that needs to be done?" she asked. "I can wash dishes if you need."

"No worries, sugar. I like doing dishes. Helps me think. You're helping me plenty by going with Rian to check on that south gate. Warren worries about everything and refuses to hire out for a darn thing. Until Kane and Laci built their house here on the property, Warren was doing everything himself and it was plumb wearing him out."

CoCo knew her father was equally stubborn about his business. He allowed very few people to have a hand in the design of the new lines, preferring to oversee every detail, almost obsessively, until they went into mass production. Even then, he insisted on touring the factories to ensure that a quality product was being churned out.

"So you and Cora Bradford were friends before she died?"

"Thick as thieves," Adeline answered with a firm nod. "She was the finest woman alive. Heart bigger than most and with a talent in the kitchen that could rival any fancy chef. She was just good at making anything she tried her hand at if it were something you put in your mouth. She always won the pie contests." She sighed with the memory. "The world lost a good one, for sure. I miss her something fierce but it's nothing compared to how Warren misses her."

"Yes, but he has you now, right?"

"Oh, honey, I'll never replace Cora and I'm okay with that. I'm just blessed to have what time I got with him."

CoCo was floored by how humble and genuinely good-hearted the woman was. It made her wish Miss Plix was still around because she had a feeling if her nanny had lived, CoCo's life would've been a lot different. For one, she wouldn't have supported the way CoCo had learned to manipulate her parents for her own gain. Suddenly ashamed, she said, "He's lucky to have you." She went to the sink and began to wash her hands, saying, "Okay, so what can I do to help? I can make sandwiches if you point me in the right direction."

"All righty! Sounds like a plan. There's some fresh roast beef and cheese in the fridge. I'll start chopping the lettuce and tomatoes. Oh, and I just picked up some of that fancy focaccia bread that will taste real yummy with that roast beef."

Within a half hour, CoCo and Adeline had fixed up a decent picnic lunch and stuffed it into a soft cooler that could be secured onto the saddle. "You have fun and enjoy yourself. It's going to be a fine day for a picnic," Adeline said, shooing her off. "I'll see you back at supper. Steaks and potatoes are on the menu tonight."

CoCo nodded and grabbed the cooler, heading out toward the barn, where Rian was supposed to be saddling the horses. She'd always loved her horses but it'd been so long since she'd actually made the time to go riding. It was amazing how less important things somehow took precedence in your life when you weren't paying attention. She entered the barn and inhaled the scent of horses and hay, a smell that'd always been so comforting to her. She found Rian with two horses, saddled and ready.

"You can have Amelia, and I'll take Dancer. They're both good, steady horses with good legs."

"Thanks," she said, handing him the picnic cooler. After they'd led their horses out of the barn, they hoisted themselves into the saddles.

CoCo glanced over at Rian and her breath caught. Why did he get sexier by the minute? There was something about the way he sat on a horse that squeezed every last bit of air from her lungs and made her stomach muscles tremble. He flashed her a smile, seeming to appreciate the way she didn't need any help, and then made a clicking noise, leading the horse out into the pasture. She did the same and they rode side by side, enjoying the cool breeze and the warm sun.

If she'd ever experienced a perfect moment in her life, this would be in the top five—and she didn't want it to end.

"As kids, Kane and I used to race each other across this field," he shared with a grin. "I was always a better rider than Kane, although the horse you're riding, Amelia, dumped me on my ass a fair number of times. She gets skittish when she's irritated."

"Oh, sure, give me the antsy horse," CoCo teased. "It's good for you that I can handle a skittish horse. My favorite horse back in Italy was a black Thoroughbred named Gypsy. She was very spirited and wouldn't let anyone else ride her but me. My dad wanted to sell her but I wouldn't let him. He was afraid that she was going to throw me and I'd break my neck but she and I had an understanding. Not that she didn't give it her best shot in the beginning. But I proved my worth and I earned the distinction of being her only rider."

"Do you still have her?"

She shook her head. "No. She got colic and we had to put her down. We tried everything but she just kept getting sicker and sicker. Finally, it was more of a mercy to put her down gently than to let her continue suffering. I never really found another horse like her. Maybe that's why I stopped riding seriously."

"It's hard to lose an animal like that. They find their way into our hearts and stay there."

She agreed, though she'd never realized before that moment that Gypsy's death had likely had something to do with the reason she'd found other pursuits. "Well, I was fifteen and I'd just started to realize the benefits of being an heiress," she admitted. "That was right about the time I talked my dad into letting me go to high school in LA. And coming home to Italy for summer and winter breaks."

"You attended LA schools?"

"Sort of. I was mostly homeschooled here in the States, and then I had a tutor back in Italy so I didn't become an 'uneducated American girl' as my father put it."

"Harsh."

"Yeah, my dad was pretty opinionated when it came to my education. Unlike my mom, who was more interested in how being homeschooled would affect my social life."

"Your mom homeschooled you?"

"God, no. She hired a teacher to come to the house."

"So what's your relationship with your mom like?"

CoCo shrugged with a sigh. "I don't know. I don't really have a relationship with her. She's too busy with her new husband to think of me. Azalea has always been a social butterfly according to my dad. That's what broke them up. He was always too busy to take her out and she felt neglected, I guess. Sometimes I think my dad wishes he'd made more of an effort but I want to tell him that he wasn't missing out on anything. My mom is inherently selfish and only thinks of herself."

"Does she know what's going on with you right now?"

"No, and I didn't see the point in telling her. She's much happier when I don't bother her with my life."

Rian wondered what his own mother would've been like. Would she have been better than his father? He tended to give her a pass because she'd died but who knows, maybe she would've been just as bad. "I'm sorry," he said, sharing a look with CoCo.

"It's okay. I no longer care about that stuff."

"I don't think we ever stop caring," he said quietly. He must've struck a nerve because she didn't offer a flip response, just accepted his comment. "You know, Warren used to tell us that how we deal with the hand we're dealt is the measure of our character. It would've been easy to use our dad's shitty example as an excuse to act up but we tried to be better than people expected of us. I know that Warren is a big part of that but my brother was determined to get out of this town and make something of himself. Warren must've seen that in him and decided to act on it. Thank God he did. He changed our lives and that's why we'd do anything for him."

"That's beautiful that you feel something so deep for him. I love my father like that. I'd do anything for him."

"So why'd you leave Italy to be with your mom, whom you don't really have a connection with?"

She sighed. "I was a young kid, dazzled by the LA lifestyle. Stupid, I know. But I was fifteen and easily impressed."

Rian knew he had to tread carefully for the next comment he was about to make but he felt it needed to be said. "Are you still easily impressed? I mean, when I first met you, you didn't come off as particularly deep. Now, granted, I didn't really know you, but your reputation... I don't know, seems to me that you came from different roots, and your foundation was a lot stronger than most."

Instead of getting angry, she appeared reflective. "True. Honestly, I don't know what happened. I got blinded by the glitz and glamour. I know it's stupid but the fast-paced lifestyle is addictive. I like having fun and when you throw a party and everyone is there, it feels as if you're loved and admired by everyone, even though deep down I think I knew that it wasn't real."

It was the most profound statement she'd made since he'd met her and he was rocked by how smart she truly was. He understood the need to fill an emotional hole with anything just to make the ache stop but he also knew that eventually nothing worked because he'd gotten to that place himself. If he were being honest, he kept his social circles superficial because he didn't want to find himself overly attached.

He risked a quick glance at CoCo, loving how the light brightened her complexion and put roses in her cheeks. Her hair, loose and free, blew in the subtle breeze and he was struck anew by how beautiful she was. She was the kind of woman model scouts snapped up because she had the face and body to make millions. And she was here with him. "Some things are real," he told her. "The love you feel for your father is genuine and he's lucky to have a daughter like you."

She cast a sweet, appreciative smile his way and he nearly fell from his horse. The emotion swelling in his chest was so powerful, it almost choked his airway. He wanted to sidle up to her and plant a kiss on those sensual lips but Kane's voice echoed in his mind, *Keep your hands off the client,* and he deliberately turned his gaze away, needing to stay focused on what was truly important.

CoCo was a temporary player in this game. His job was to keep her alive.

Yeah, so try to remember that.

15

THEY KEPT AN easy pace for about an hour and then crested a beautiful rolling hill when Rian pointed at the gate. "There's the south gate. Watch as you come down the hill."

"I could handle this terrain at five years old." To emphasize her point, she spurred Amelia into a run, laughing with abandon as the wind whipped her hair and she left Rian in the dust. Amelia had good legs and within seconds they were galloping down the gentle slope and into a grassy meadow. Her heart light, she came skidding to a stop as they reached the gate. She reached down and patted Amelia's damp neck, crooning with approval. "You're a good girl. I bet you could handle even more than that, can't you?" She straightened and Rian sidled up to her, his eyes flashing with good humor, and she sent him a saucy grin. "I win."

"No fair. I didn't know we were racing until you shot off like a bat out of hell. Nice riding, by the way. You weren't kidding when you said you were comfortable on a horse."

"Did you think I was lying?"

"Well, maybe not lying but perhaps stretching the truth a bit. I mean, city girls aren't usually ones for riding in the country."

"Well, I'm only *part* city girl."

"I see that." He slid from his horse and grabbed his tools from the saddlebag to check the gate. She watched as he lifted the gate and started hammering the hinge. His biceps bulged with each clanging hit on the metal and she found herself shifting in the saddle, very aware of her body. "This shouldn't take too long. If you want to pick a spot for lunch, that'd be good," he said.

She nodded and slid from Amelia, giving the pretty horse a playful rub on the nose before unpacking the picnic cooler and the blanket strapped to the horse's flank. She spread the gingham woolen blanket and began to unpack the cooler, humming to herself as she went. Birds flitted from the trees and bees buzzed. The metal clanging sounded out of place with the beautiful landscape, but CoCo was delirious with the simple joy of the moment. Nothing was perfect but this moment came pretty damn close.

Once she had all the fixings laid out, roast beef sandwiches, chips, drinks and even a few oatmeal raisin cookies, she waited for Rian, who followed a few minutes later. He took a nice, long swig from his water bottle and then plopped down beside her. "So I hope you like roast beef because that's what's on the menu," she said, suddenly a little nervous, though why she didn't know.

"Sounds great," he said, grabbing his sandwich and taking a hearty bite. There was something that tickled her insides—something so feminine—about making a meal for Rian, though she'd never been one to appreciate domestic stereotypes before. However, now that she thought about it, her father hadn't exactly been a feminist—he'd always preferred female cooks in the kitchen because he said they just knew more about making good food than men. So yeah, maybe her dad was a male chauvinist and she'd never noticed! She giggled at the uncomfortable thought and caught Rian's puzzled stare as he chewed. "Something funny about roast beef that I'm unaware of?" he asked.

"No, I was just—randomly—thinking of my father and how he might be a male chauvinist, but in the nicest way possible. He doesn't believe in putting women down or anything like that but he does play into the gender stereotype a bit."

"How so?"

"Well, all our cooks were always female. He said that women inherently knew what to do in the kitchen because it was in their blood."

"All the executive male chefs in the world might have something to say about that."

She shrugged. "I know. That's why I giggled. I just never realized that about my father."

"There could be another reason your dad hired only women…" He wagged his eyebrows and she laughed. He shrugged. "Just pointing out the obvious."

"The cooks were always plump, older and a little bossy. Kind of like Adeline."

"Hey, I'm not here to judge," he said, trying to hide a laugh, and she playfully pushed at his shoulder. "Each to his own right?"

"Eww, I don't want to talk about my dad's love life. And no, he wasn't chasing after the cooks." They ate in companionable silence and then CoCo broke a cookie in half and handed him the other half. He accepted it with a smile and gobbled it down. Then he shocked her when he scooped up the other cookie and gobbled it down just as quickly, giving her a cheeky grin when she gasped and tackled him. "We were supposed to share!" she said, laughing when she landed on top of him. His arms wound around her and he looked adorable lying in the sunshine, the light playing with the highlights in his subtle waves. "Are you always such a pig when it comes to cookies?"

"Always," he said without a hint of apology, his grin widening. "It's one of my flaws."

She smiled and brushed her lips across his, murmuring, "I guess you're entitled to one or two…" and then she deepened the kiss, needing desperately to taste him again, to feel him moving inside her. His tongue swept her mouth and she climbed on top of him, remembering the last time she was in this position, and she deepened the kiss, getting more aroused by the second. This time would be different because he wasn't doped up. She wanted to experience sex with Rian when he was in full control of his faculties.

His touch became more urgent and he rolled her onto her back, his hips and groin matching up with hers with delicious pressure in all the right places. But just as things were beginning to get to the point where clothes were going to fly, he slowed with a groan and pulled away, rolling to his back to stare into the sky, agitated.

"What's wrong?" she asked, confused. "Was it something I did?"

He shook his head. "No, we can't do this."

She frowned. "Why not? We're both consenting adults."

"You're a client." He sat up, scooting back. That tiny bit of distance hurt her feelings. One minute he was all over her and now she had the plague? "I don't mess with clients."

Maybe he thought his explanation would soften the blow but it hadn't. She blinked back tears and tried to play it off that he hadn't just punched her emotionally. "So the only reason you slept with me the other night was because of the drug," she said, as if it was no big deal. "I get it. Sure."

He groaned. "I wish it were that easy." He turned to her and tried to explain but she didn't want to hear it. What difference did it make why he didn't want to be with her? He caught the shake of her head and pulled her abruptly back to his mouth, shocking her with the sudden movement. He took her mouth with the same intensity as a man who might die tomorrow, with a faint air of desperation tinged with anger at the world, and she happily drank in the sensation of drowning in his urgent touch.

There was something to be said for ignoring all the reasons why you shouldn't and just embracing the fact that it's going to happen. And she was good with that.

THE LITTLE VOICE that managed to stop him in the beginning was fading fast under the sensual onslaught of CoCo's touch. She was like ambrosia and he couldn't get enough. Her skin glowed in the bright sunshine and he was already working up a sweat in anticipation of tasting those rose nipples again, loving the way they tightened and pearled beneath his tongue, the breathy rasps of her voice as he brought her to a shuddering end. His arms felt empty without her in them and he couldn't blame the drug this time. But what was he doing? He could practically hear Kane's censure, the heavy weight of disappointment weighing on him for deliberately ignoring the good sense screaming at him to stop.

But stopping was the last thing he wanted to do. His hands shook with the need to feel her naked skin against his. There was something incredibly hot about the idea of sex in this field with CoCo, something that plucked at a previously unknown exhibitionist streak that revved his engine hard.

CoCo frantically tore at his shirt, shoving it off his shoulders and practically tearing it from his body with a sexy growl that made his blood race. She bit at his shoulder with a giggle and pinched his nipple as she rose up to claim his mouth again. God, she was so damn hot. She was both dominant and submissive. The two divergent qualities working in tandem cranked his gears until he was practically blowing steam from his ears. He couldn't touch enough of her to feel satisfaction. A never-ending hunger to know her body, to wring those sweet gasps and cries from her mouth, drove him mercilessly until they were both naked, panting and desperate to feel one another.

He reared up, his cock bobbing with eagerness for that willing, slick heat, but he had the wherewithal to briefly pause with a tortured gasp to ask, "Are you…? I don't have any condoms…"

"You silly boy, I'm on the pill. What do you take me for?" She grinned and pulled him down, sucking in a wild breath as he thrust into her, his thick length sliding in easily until he was buried so deeply inside her that he was surely touching her womb. "Oh, Rian…" That breathy cry thrilled him to his core as he moved slowly against her, building the friction to unbearably pleasurable levels.

"God, yes…yes! That's it…just like that…" She wiggled against him, moaning, and he grinned, using one hand to grasp her arms and stretch them above her head, holding her there while he pumped into her. She bucked, moaning loudly, and he took pride in the fact that he was doing the job right. He angled his hips as she lifted hers and he hit that spot hard and suddenly she gushed with a guttural cry, her nipples tightening so hard that they pointed to the sky, begging for a mouth to suck on them. He wanted to oblige but he was too focused on watching the pleasure build in her beautiful face.

"R-Rian, oh, my God, *R-R-Rian*!" And then she shattered apart, everything clenching inside, gripping his cock with her internal muscles as they coaxed his own orgasm with each tightening band. He lost control, his thrusts became erratic and suddenly her sweet core was milking the juice right out of his body. He filled her, shuddering as he emptied. He collapsed and rolled to the side, sweat rolling down his bare back as the warm sunshine quickly dried his wet, softening cock and he closed his eyes, barely able to breathe.

That was the most epic sex he'd ever experienced.

Far better than the drug-induced hard-on from hell.

Hell, far better than any carnal activity he'd ever participated in since he'd first discovered sex.

And now that he'd gone and done the one thing he said he wouldn't…what happened now?

He didn't know. He was out of his depth. What was it about CoCo that made him throw out all the rules and do what he knew he shouldn't?

He didn't want to be like all the other guys she strung

along for her entertainment. But then, he didn't want a relationship, either. So what was going on between them? Something dangerous, that much he knew.

Maybe he ought to tell her this was a bad idea and they couldn't do it again. He ought to put his foot down and just say the words even if he didn't quite mean them. But the fact was, he wanted to do it again and again and again. Hell, if they could spend the rest of their time in Kentucky screwing each other raw, he'd be okay with that. And that was a terrible idea!

Even knowing that, he knew the words wouldn't cross his lips. He wanted CoCo in the worst way and having her had only increased his appetite for more.

You done it now, boy.

Not even the echo of his older brother's voice was enough to snap him out of this dangerous mind-set.

He had to figure things out.

But it wasn't going to happen today, that was for damn sure.

16

"YOUR BRAIN IS on fire, isn't it?" she asked, rolling to her stomach to regard Rian, who'd gone silent. They were still naked as the day they were born but neither was in a rush to get dressed. "Tell me what you're thinking."

He smiled. "Isn't that a little dangerous?"

"I'm brave. Go ahead, try me."

Rian laughed. "I think I just did."

CoCo giggled and rose up to brush a playful kiss across his lips. "You know what I mean. I promise I won't bite."

"What if I like it when you bite?" he asked with a half grin twisting his mouth. "I mean, there's something to be said for a little nibble here and there."

"C'mon, tell me what's on your mind. I know you're probably dealing with some kind of guilt, right?"

He nodded with a chagrined chuckle. "And here I thought I was mysterious."

"No, not really," she said, shaking her head. "Sorry to burst your bubble."

He sighed and rose up on his elbows. "Okay, yeah, I'm feeling guilty because I just broke my own rule about messing around with a client. I mean, I could forgive myself for the first time because I was under the influence of something, but I can't use that excuse this time."

"Are you saying you need an excuse to have sex with me?" she asked, raising a brow. "Because that doesn't make me feel very good. And neither does the idea that you're just 'messing around' with me. Makes me feel… you know, cheap."

"No, not like that, I'm sorry," he rushed to clarify. "It's just that I have rules in place for a reason and they're good reasons. I deal with celebrity clients all the time. It's my job to protect the reputation of the company by remaining professional at all times, even when the client is dead-sexy and hotter than Georgia asphalt."

His frank comment thrilled her. A slow smile formed. "Are you saying that *I'm* hotter than Georgia asphalt?"

"You know you are," he growled, pulling her so that she straddled him. "You're the hottest woman I've ever laid eyes on."

"You know what they say about rules… They're meant to be broken."

His hands filled with her breasts, his gaze darkening as he gently squeezed the plump flesh. A small groan escaped as he rose up, tucking her legs around his torso and suddenly grabbing a handful of her ass. "Some rules, yes. Others, no."

"Says who?"

"Says me. If word got out that I was sleeping with a client, we wouldn't get more jobs. This is our livelihood. I couldn't do that to Kane."

She appreciated how much integrity Rian had. It was a refreshing change from the usual people she hung out with but that didn't mean she was going to suddenly stop wanting to have sex with him. "How about this… while we are here at the ranch, we do whatever we want with each other but once we leave…we'll pretend that nothing ever happened."

He eyed her curiously. "That would work for you?"

"Sure. As cute as you are, I'm not sure a relationship would really work out, but we have the kind of chemistry that's hard to deny so why should we if we don't have to? At least for the moment, right?"

He was beginning to warm to her logic. "So, you're okay with having sex all day long while we're here but the minute we leave, it's cold turkey between us?"

"A frozen turkey," she promised, though a small part of her wondered if that were actually possible. Their chemistry was off the charts. It might be hard to just shut it off. But she'd deal with that later. Right now, she'd say or do anything to get Rian to agree to her idea.

She wiggled against him, her wet core sliding across his cock, reminding him of what he'd done to her. His gaze flared with instant lust and she sucked in a wild breath as she felt his cock stirring to life. Damn, his stamina was incredible. "Careful, country boy, don't start the engine if you're not ready to drive," she taunted him with a sweet, daring smile. Oh, that was like throwing gasoline on a fire! She laughed as he buried his face against her neck, sucking the soft skin of her shoulder, and they tumbled to the blanket, completely comfortable with one another as they quickly banged out round two, leaving them both breathless and barely able to move by the end. At this rate, riding her horse back to the ranch was going to be a challenge.

But she didn't care. There was something about Rian Dalton that she couldn't get enough of.

A voice at the back of her mind warned that this could become a problem. But CoCo had discovered she could effectively drown out her inner voice with epic bouts of sex, which was exactly what she planned to do with the very willing, very sexy country boy at her disposal.

Yeehah!

BY THE TIME they returned to the ranch, it was nearing four o'clock and they had to hustle to shower and get ready for supper. Of course, a shower necessitated nudity and nudity encouraged monkey business, so the shower took a bit longer than usual but Rian wasn't complaining. In fact, when he remembered what CoCo had done to him in the shower, he nearly blushed.

He was almost in awe of the woman's sexual skills and that was saying a lot. He wasn't a prude by any means but that woman...she made him feel like a teenager without a lick of practical knowledge. It was sexy and intimidating at the same time but he wanted more.

"How'd you learn that little trick?" he asked, bracketing CoCo against the bathroom wall as she was drying off. "That was pretty epic."

"Europeans are less squeamish about sex," she answered with a shrug and a smile. "My first lover was an older man. He taught me a few things."

Rian pushed off, intrigued. "How much older?"

"Old enough." She dropped her towel and he momentarily forgot what he was talking about and she switched subjects. "So what's going to happen at this dinner? I think for the sake of appearances we should keep things professional, easier to avoid awkward questions that way. Do you agree?"

"Yeah, sure," he said, not caring about dinner. He wanted to know more about this older guy. "So, when you say *older*, what does that mean? Was he, like, some old man?"

She cast an irritated look his way. "Really? Does it matter?"

"Yeah, kinda."

"Oh, my God, you're being a baby. Do you really want details about something that never concerned you?" When he remained stubbornly silent, she rolled her eyes and shimmied into her sundress, saying, "Okay, I was seventeen, he was forty-two. He was a business associate of my father's and I met him on his yacht. We had chemistry and we acted on it. Discreetly, of course. End of story. We did our thing for about two months and then we parted ways without harsh feelings. It's not as if I was looking to marry the man. I enjoyed that he was a generous lover and he was far more attentive than any of the silly boys trying to get my attention who didn't know what to do with a hole in the ground."

Why was he jealous of some guy from her past? What did it matter? "That's quite an age gap," he said, unable to help himself. "I mean, if it'd happened in the States, he could've gone to jail because it's illegal."

"Well, it wasn't here. Can we drop it?"

"Yeah, I guess."

"Good. I'm starved." She rose up on her tiptoes and kissed him, then said, "If it matters, as good as it was with him, it's so much better with you and I'm not just saying that to soothe your ego. If the sex wasn't electric between us, I wouldn't waste my time."

That did help a little. He allowed a smile and surprised her by hoisting her onto his hips. She smiled as she hooked her legs around his torso. "We have time for a quickie," he said and she laughed, assuming he wasn't serious, but right now he was already hard and ready. To illustrate that point, he pressed her against the wall and pushed his erection against her. "See? I'm ready if you are."

"Tempting," she groaned but shook her head. "I'm not about to formally meet your family with sex hair. Cool your jets, country boy."

He let her down with a reluctant sigh and attempted to shift his boner into a less obvious position. "All right, princess. But all bets are off as soon as we get back."

She cast him a devilish grin. "Don't make promises you can't keep."

"I don't." *That's right, baby. I'm going to ruin you for other men.* "C'mon, let's get over there before Adeline sends a search party," he growled, wanting nothing more than to blow off dinner so he could feast on CoCo, but he'd never do that to Warren and Adeline. But just as CoCo was about to open the front door, he jerked her into his arms for a searing kiss that left them both breathless. "Something to tide me over until dinner is over," he said, burning holes into her with his need to touch her.

She nodded, her lips glistening, her eyes wide, and then he turned her loose. When her gait was slightly tipsy, his ego swelled in proportion to his eager cock. *Yeah, nice to see that that road traveled both ways.*

He loved Adeline and Warren with all his heart but right about now, he wanted to skip dinner and go straight to dessert.

17

"Oh, look at you," Adeline gushed, ushering them into the kitchen with effusive hugs for them both. "You are so beautiful. Rian, you better scoop up this pretty thing before someone else with more sense does."

CoCo blushed and wondered how uncomfortable that made Rian, but when she snuck a glance at him she saw something that shocked her—contemplation—as if Adeline's advice had struck a nerve, and her stomach trembled at the thought. No, neither of them was looking for a relationship. This was just good times and she was fine with that. Besides, it wasn't as if either of their lifestyles was conducive to having a permanent plus one. For starters, Rian would hate her friends. He certainly didn't have anything nice to say about Stella, not that CoCo blamed him, but it would make things awkward when she wanted to party with them. "Smells amazing," she said, hoping to redirect the older woman.

"Oh! Yes, steaks and mashed potatoes, corn on the cob, that's what we make around here, stuff that will stick to your ribs. Good country food. And the steaks are from our own cattle. Nothing fresher than that."

"Have you ever had fresh milk?" Rian asked.

She surprised him with an eager nod. "We had a farmer who would deliver fresh eggs and milk every day in exchange for a new pair of shoes every six months. The farmer had a taste for fine shoes when he went out but he couldn't afford my dad's shoes so my dad worked out a barter with him. It suited them both."

"That sounds like a good ol' country arrangement between good folk," Adeline said, approving just as Warren walked in.

The older man was spry, in good shape and hearty like most men who worked with their hands for a living. She sensed his innate integrity and felt immensely grateful to this man for giving the Dalton boys a reason to hope when they needed it the most. Unexpected tears sprang from an unknown place and she had to push them back with a sunny smile as she introduced herself. "I'm CoCo Abelli. Thank you so much for allowing me to stay while things are worked out with my father. It means so much to have a safe place to hide."

"Don't even think about it," he said gruffly as he took his place at the head of the table. "Bradford Ranch is a safe haven."

She smiled with true gratitude because that's exactly what this place felt like—a safe haven. Maybe it was because of Rian but she couldn't imagine being anywhere but here at the moment. "Your ranch is amazing. What a beautiful piece of land you have."

"Isn't it, though?" Adeline agreed as she ladled mashed potatoes onto her plate. "When I first saw it, forty some years ago, I was in awe. Truth be told, I was a bit jealous of Cora and her good fortune. She managed to land the best man in all of Kentucky and she got this amazing property to tend. But no one deserved it more than Warren and Cora. Good people."

CoCo smiled at Adeline's open generosity and marveled at how easy she was with admitting her own faults, even if they were from forty years ago. Everything about Adeline was sweet and unassuming. It made her wish she'd been able to meet this legendary Cora, as well. It also made her miss Miss Plix all the more, which was interesting because before all this, she'd shamefully forgotten about the older woman.

"Tell me about this pickle you're in, young lady," Warren said, tucking into his steak. "Rian tells me your father is being threatened and the FBI are involved. Are they any closer to solving the case?"

She looked to Rian. "I don't know. We're removed from the investigation. Rian is keeping me safe while the FBI do their thing."

"I talked with the agent in charge and he said they were close to finding who was responsible. I'm sure it won't take long now."

Was it bad that she was disappointed? If the feds were close to nailing the bad guy, that meant that Rian's services wouldn't be required for much longer. CoCo swallowed the meat stuck in her throat and realized that put a damper on her mood. *Snap out of it. You set up the perimeters and you knew this was temporary. Grab your bliss, while you can.* She forced a bright smile. "Tell me about Rian. What was he like growing up? Was he always such a charmer?"

Adeline hooted with laughter, eager to share. "Oh, the stories Cora would tell about this young man. Of course, don't tell Kane but this boy right here always stole her heart! She would say, 'Heaven help the lady who finally catches this boy's eye because he's worth putting up with all the shenanigans he does.'"

"Hey now, no throwing me under the bus, Miss Adeline," Rian warned with a half-serious glower. "Can I help it that the ladies dig me?"

"Tell me more about this little country player," teased CoCo, enjoying how Rian was beginning to squirm.

Warren decided to get in on the fun. "There was this little gal down the road who had the biggest crush on Rian. She'd come around every day and try to get his attention and boy, she finally succeeded. Next thing I know, he's asking for extra chores so he can earn a little more. Little vixen had talked him into going to some school dance. I never seen him so determined to buy some gal a fancy bouquet for her wrist. But he did it. Earned every penny."

"Aw, what a sweet boy," CoCo crooned, giggling as Rian rolled his eyes and looked ready to crawl under the table with embarrassment. "But that doesn't surprise me. Rian is quite the gentleman when he chooses to be."

And quite the animal under the right circumstances. Rian met her gaze and a heated moment passed between them. *Oh, damn. Don't go thinking about that or you'll never make it through dinner.*

Rian effectively changed the subject, saying, "I fixed the south gate. Just needed a little adjustment on the hinge. Now it swings open easily."

"Good, good," Warren grunted with appreciation. "Been meaning to get out there but time got away from me. Any other problems with the fencing on that side?"

"Nope. Kane did a good job of mending it."

"Kane's a good man. Glad to have him around more. So you think you might be coming around more often?"

Warren asked, putting Rian on the spot. "There's plenty of acreage for another house."

"I'd love to but someone has to keep the business running smoothly and to do that I have to be in LA."

"I understand. Just miss having you around is all."

"And I miss being here," he said with genuine emotion and CoCo was envious of the obvious connection between them. The lack of DNA meant nothing between these two; they were plainly family and that warmed her heart. "So when are you and Adeline gonna tie the knot?" Rian asked.

Adeline tittered and said, "We rather like living in sin. Seems so…I don't know…exciting. But our pastor is none too pleased, that's for sure. Thankfully, I keep him supplied with pies and he forgives us."

Warren cracked a reluctant smile and CoCo just wanted to hug both of them. They were good people, whether they were living in sin or not, and their goodness had nothing to do with how many times they went to church. She liked that. She needed more of this in her life and less of…everything else her life had been comprised of up until this moment.

Deep stuff to contemplate over a plate of country mashed potatoes.

Deep, indeed.

AFTER DINNER AND some more chatting, they said their goodbyes and made their way back to Kane's place, Rian barely able to keep his hands to himself. It was dark, except for the sparkle of the stars overhead and the fireflies buzzing lazily here and there. The night was warm but not overly so. He would be more than happy to ditch his clothes but CoCo had different plans.

"Do you ever swim in the pond?" she asked, gesturing to the huge pond on the property that Warren always had stocked with fish because fishing relaxed him. It was far enough from the house that Rian and Kane used to splash around without worrying that they'd wake the Bradfords when they decided to go midnight frogging.

"I used to when I was a kid. It's plenty deep so the water's clean. Nothing worse than brackish pond water, right?"

She laughed. "I wouldn't know." She tugged at his hand. "Let's go put our feet in."

"Why?" he asked, more interested in getting CoCo beneath him than playing splashy-splashy in the water. "I have something better in mind."

"So do I." And then she shocked him by stripping as she walked away from him, her dress landing in a heap on the grass as she walked gloriously naked to the small pier. She waved and then dived into the water. She popped from the surface with a gasp, laughing as she exclaimed, "It's a little chillier than I thought it would be. Come warm me up, country boy."

Crazy woman. He grinned and kicked his boots free, unbuttoning his shirt as he went. "I could've told you that," he said, shucking his pants and then taking a running leap and landing in the water beside her. He reached for her and pulled her naked body into his arms, treading water with her holding on to him. He kissed her long and deep, loving the feel of CoCo against him. "You're always surprising me," he shared as he broke the kiss. Her eyes sparkled in the night air and her sweet smile lit up his heart. "Just when I think I have you figured out, you go and do something to turn my head inside out."

"Good," CoCo murmured, leaning back as Rian supported her. Her full breasts crested the water's surface as if kissing the moon and he bit back a groan of pure desire as his cock began to harden. She rose slowly, her hair dripping down her back, and reached down to squeeze his growing erection. "Hmm, Mr. Dalton, we have a situation," she said with a husky laugh.

"And what situation would that be?"

"Sex is difficult to manage underwater."

He laughed and swam over to the shore, carrying her as he went until he climbed from the water, her legs tucked around his waist and her arms looped around his neck.

"A girl could get used to this," she whispered and his heart skipped a beat, but not in the way that would've sent a warning down his spine. No, this was different and would be even more worrisome if he were thinking clearly.

He laid her gently on the ground and joined her, wasting no time in covering her sweet, lithe body with his, loving how his angles matched her curves. "Rian," she breathed, his name like a prayer on her lips. He moved down her belly, pressing tiny kisses on the bare skin, causing goose bumps to riot, and then delved into that sweet place that he couldn't get enough of.

"You taste so good," he murmured, parting her folds gently and dipping his tongue to lap at the tiny, responsive nub. Her breathy moans and cries spurred him on and he listened to the changes in her breathing to know when to speed up or slow down. Within five minutes, her thighs began to shake and she stuffed a fist into her mouth to keep from screaming and he knew he'd hit the right spot. He rose with a satisfied grin, his pride swelling in concert with his cock as she rocked on her hips, squeezing her thighs together with a heavy moan as her orgasm slowly receded.

"You are pretty talented with that tongue," she admitted, her voice a little scratchy, suddenly grinning wildly. "Challenge accepted." And then she latched onto his cock and the tables were reversed. She sucked and teased, gripping his balls with a tender but firm touch, nibbling at the sensitive head and nipping now and then, which caused him to jerk, and then when he thought he couldn't handle another minute, she added her hands to the mix and then he was lost, coming so hard he nearly fell down, his knees buckling.

He felt fevered and flushed but definitely satisfied. He dropped to his butt, joining her on the soft grass, and then fell back with a thump. She joined him with a sigh, cuddling up to his shoulder as if she were always meant to be there. They stayed a moment just listening to the night sounds, watching as the fireflies buzzed and the pond water lapped at the shore. She broke the silence first. "What was it like growing up here?" she asked.

It was sanctuary. He sighed. "Well, we didn't meet the Bradfords until we were young teens. Before that, we were stuck with the old man and growing up with him was shit."

"How'd you get your dad to agree to let you stay with the Bradfords?"

"We paid him off. Kane knew the only way to get our dad to sign off on letting us stay the summer was if we were working and we gave up a percentage of our cash. We lied about how much we were making and then gave the bastard fifteen percent of our cash each week. It was enough to keep him in booze and that's all he cared about anyway so he left us alone."

She fell silent, digesting the information, then said, "That was pretty smart to pay him off."

Her praise lifted the sudden crushing oppression memories of his dad always evoked. "It was Kane's idea," he admitted. "But yeah, Kane was pretty smart to think of it. Kane was always fast on his feet. Except when it came to Laci." He chuckled at the memory of how stupidly stubborn Kane had been when Laci was involved. "He got it into his head that Laci was better off without him tagging along so he left her. Broke her heart. Went and joined the military. It was a stupid move but he had good intentions. It took years before they found each other again."

"Kinda romantic," CoCo said, sighing. "Star-crossed lovers."

"Well, if you'd been around when they were yelling at each other, you might not say that. They have tempers and Laci is pure country. She can give as good as she gets."

"I wish I could meet her."

The wistful comment twisted something inside him and he tightened his hold on her because he knew it wasn't likely that CoCo and Laci would ever meet. It wasn't as if they traveled in the same circles. "You'd like her. She's down-to-earth, very nice considering she's a megastar, but then I've never looked at her like that. I still remember when she was a wild country girl, running around in pigtails and overalls, barefoot and free. Now she's all famous but she's just Laci to me. Kinda like a little sister."

"You mean you never had a crush on her?"

"Nah, she always had eyes for Kane and I just never saw her like that. I love her and always will but she's Kane's girl and always will be."

"Now, that's romantic," CoCo said, rising on her elbow. "Have you ever been in love?"

He shook his head. "No," he answered, pausing to ask about the guy she wouldn't share earlier at the bar. "Tell me about the guy you fell in love with."

She sighed at the memory. "It's kind of embarrassing. I mistakenly thought that this guy was into me but I found out later that he was playing a game with me and two other girls. I dumped him as soon as I found out. You might know him. He's the lead singer of a famous band. Although at the time, he was just singing in his parents' garage—badly, I might add—and having trouble booking gigs."

"Who is it?" he asked, curiosity getting the better of him.

She bit her lip. "Promise not to laugh?"

"No," he answered with a cheeky grin and she swatted at him. "Okay, okay, I promise. Who was it?"

She took a deep breath and answered with a slight cringe, "Jeremiah Stinger."

"From Not Another Garage Band?" When she nodded, he tried to hold back his laughter but wasn't very successful.

"Hey! That's not nice. I was only nineteen and didn't know any better. But in my defense, he used to be hot and I didn't know he was such a douche until I caught him in bed with another girl, a groupie, of all clichéd things."

"Yeah, musicians…they're kinda all the same in my experience. I've had a few as clients. I think I prefer politicians over musicians and I *hate* politicians. There's only so many times you can pretend you aren't in the same room as someone getting a blowjob. Just awkward."

She wrinkled her nose. "Really?"

"Oh, yeah. I've seen things that have really left a mental scar. That's why I prefer not to deal with musicians. Groupies are a pain in the ass."

"Have you ever been offered sexual favors?"

He laughed. "Of course. Which is why the easiest rule to keep things straight is not to mess with clients—or the groupies of clients."

She snuggled against him. "Poor you. Having to fend off blowjobs."

"True story. Rough life."

CoCo squealed with giggles as he grabbed her and began tickling, laughing himself as they rolled around, still completely naked—and neither minded. It was a perfect moment that he didn't want to end.

Funny, lately, there'd been quite a few of those.

18

IT WAS THE DAY after Rian had finished helping Warren with the cattle and CoCo had helped Adeline do a little grocery shopping in the tiny town of Woodsville that Rian and CoCo found themselves back on the horses, enjoying a leisurely ride through the countryside.

"I'd forgotten how much I enjoy riding," she admitted, loving the clean country air and the carefree feeling in her heart. "I used to love it."

"Warren used to say that wisdom could always be found in the company of a good horse."

She laughed, agreeing. "He's right. I lost all my wisdom once we had to put Gypsy down. For a brief moment I'd considered getting a new horse but each time I tried, I started crying. Suddenly, partying and going out with friends seemed so much more fun than dealing with my grief."

"At least a horse won't slip something in your drink," he noted derisively and she supposed he was right. She should've stuck with horses. "Speaking of, what's the deal with that friend of yours, Stella?"

CoCo sighed. "I don't know. She's a party girl. She

loves a good time and isn't afraid to go after one. I think that's what I liked most about her when we first met. Believe it or not, I was a little shy when I first moved back to live with my mom. I didn't really know anyone and Stella helped me break out of my shell."

"Did you go to college?"

"Of course. Honor roll with a degree in marketing."

"Wow. Impressive."

She laughed wistfully. "Now ask me what I've done with that degree and you'll be a lot less impressed."

"So what happened?"

"Life happened, I guess. Getting a job was a lot less attractive than being footloose and fancy-free, plus no one was making me do anything so I didn't. My mom couldn't care less about what I do and my dad is so sweet and understanding that he never pushes me to do anything."

"So why marketing?"

"My dad wants me to take over the company."

"Do you want to?"

At one time she thought it would be exciting to work for the company that her father had built from the ground up but then working in general had lost its appeal and she'd stopped thinking about it at all. "I don't know. I mean, it's shoes, you know? I wanted to design a women's shoe line but my dad was insistent that I stick to the menswear. I just didn't have an interest. Eventually, I stopped sketching my own ideas and discarded the idea of working for my dad at all."

"What did you sketch?"

She blushed at the idea of sharing something so personal. Sure, they'd had sex but that had nothing to do with her dreams and ambitions. Somehow sharing her private sketches felt so much more intimate. "Nothing really, just doodles of heels and whatnot."

"Are you any good?" he asked and she stared, incredulous at his unapologetic question. He shrugged. "Hey, that I like to sing in the shower doesn't mean I can belt out a hit like Laci can."

"Okay, fair point and, um, I think I might be good. Well, I don't know, maybe I suck," she said, blushing. "I see the lines in my head of how a shoe should conform to the foot and... Never mind, it's stupid."

"It's not stupid. It's pretty cool, actually."

"Really? You think so?"

"I wouldn't say otherwise. One thing about me, princess, I never shoot bull for the sake of shooting it. I don't have the time to keep lies straight."

CoCo bit her lip to keep from smiling. She liked that Rian was honest. It was such a breath of fresh air after hanging out with so many liars. "Anyway, I stopped trying and my dad stopped asking."

"Seems like you're ignoring your calling."

"Maybe. But I never really thought designing shoes was very glamorous. I mean, it's a shoe. I love my dad and I'm very proud of him but designing shoes is just... I don't know...a little boring."

"No? What about Stella McCartney? She has a shoe line, right?"

"Of course."

"Well, I don't think anyone's accusing her of being less than glamorous. I mean, she hangs with Gwennie, am I right?"

At that CoCo giggled. "I never took you for a name-dropper."

"I use whatever I can get to make a point. Seriously, though. Why'd you really quit?"

She sighed, the question hitting a raw spot. "I don't know. The pressure, I guess. You can't fail if you don't try, right? I mean, my dad never questioned that I would follow in his footsteps but what if I can't handle the weight of his expectations? I mean, what if I'm not as good as him and I ruin the company?"

"It could happen," he agreed pragmatically and she rose up to stare at him with a frown. Wasn't he supposed to reassure her that she was being silly and that everything would be fine? Oh, that's right, he didn't like to lie. Well, she took back her previous thought that honesty was refreshing.

He chuckled and said, "Calm down, tigress. All I'm saying is that, true, you could fail. That's part of the risk when you try something new. But there's the opposite of failing, as well. You could rock and you could be better than your dad ever was. If the pendulum swings one way, it has to swing the other because the world is about balance."

"Very Zen of you," she said drily but he had a point. "But I don't want to take the chance of failing my father. He worked his entire life building his company. It means everything to him."

"And the fact that he believes in you as strongly as he does his company says a lot about how he feels about you." She bowed her head, blinking back tears. She knew her father was nuts about her. She'd used his love for her more times than she was proud of to get what she wanted. Manipulation was a sport you medaled in in the circles she traveled. Maybe it was time for different circles?

Rian gathered her in his arms with a soft sigh. "Don't sweat the small stuff, kid. And it's all small stuff, right? You're talented, so do something with it. What if Laci had listened to all the haters who'd said she was nothing but a backwater country girl with a guitar? She thumbed her nose at all of them and look at her now, racking up hit songs and taking names like a champ."

CoCo sniffed with a watery laugh. "That's true." She'd love to meet Laci but that was looking too far into the future to tackle right now. She turned and Rian responded by giving her a quick but sweet kiss that melted her from the inside out. "You're such a good kisser," she murmured. *I'm going to miss this.* A sharp pang punctuated the thought and she said, "Let's go back inside before we scare the wildlife," if only to give herself something to do to collect herself. If she stayed in this spot, cuddled up to Rian for much longer, she'd start bawling.

"Done and done," he said, grinning as he helped her up. They quickly donned their discarded clothing and walked hand in hand back to the house like an old married couple. It felt right. It felt like a fairy tale. It felt like more than just something to pass the time.

And her heart wouldn't likely let her forget.

19

THE NEXT DAY Rian found CoCo in the kitchen, trying her hand at an apple pie, and he grinned at how perplexed she seemed rolling out the pie dough. She looked up, exasperated. "This is impossible. The dough keeps breaking off and crumbling. I can't get it to roll into a nice sheet like the YouTube video!"

He couldn't help himself and kissed her because she was damn adorable and completely out of her depth but she was giving it a whirl, anyway. That spoke to character and spunk—two things he appreciated in a woman. Well, that and the fact that she was incredibly hot in her booty shorts and pink-and-white tank. What red-blooded American male wouldn't appreciate the sight of CoCo in the kitchen? "Just ask Adeline, she'd be happy to help you out."

"No way. I wanted to do this on my own. I didn't think this would be so hard, honestly."

"A good pie crust is part of a baker's secret weapon. Laci was the only one Cora shared her secret ingredient with. That's how guarded her recipe was."

CoCo's expression crumpled into despair. "What was

I thinking? This was stupid." She rolled up the dough and started to toss it into the garbage but he rescued it in time with a "Hey, hey! Let's not be too hasty!" and she glared, a smudge of flour on her nose. "This is dumb. I'm not cut out for domestic stuff. I don't even know why I thought I would be."

"It just takes practice. Lucky for you, I picked up a few skills while abroad," he said, winking. "Okay, so the problem here is you need more moisture. A little bit of cold water, just a bit, will fix that right up." To demonstrate, he added a teaspoon of cold water to the dough and then began to lightly work it in, careful not to overwork it. Suddenly, the dough was much more pliable and actually started to cooperate.

"I love pie," he admitted sheepishly when CoCo just stared at him with a slightly befuddled expression. "What? A badass like myself isn't allowed to express himself with pie? Baking relaxes me."

"Any other hidden talents I might like to know about?" she asked with a teasing smile that made him want to kiss it right off her lips.

"That's on a need-to-know basis," he said with a mock stern expression. "The United States government is counting on me to keep certain skills under wraps."

She rolled her eyes. "Okay, *Benny* Crocker. You can keep your secrets. Just help me with this pie."

He jumped in, showing her the best way to roll out the dough and lay it into the pie dish, and then helped her finish up the filling. He was just setting the timer when he heard Dundee attempt to bay, but the sound that came out was more like the honks out of a strangled tuba than a barking dog.

CoCo cringed along with Rian. "That's not natural,"

he said and CoCo agreed. "Must mean someone pulled up in the driveway. Hold on, I'll check it out."

Rian pushed open the screen door and saw Kane emerge from the truck. "What are you doing back from Montana already?" he asked, perplexed and concerned that they'd cut short their trip on his account. "Everything okay?"

"Actually, we got there and after the first night, the plumbing exploded during a hard freeze and then the cabin was inhabitable. There weren't any other cabins available to rent and since we didn't want to spend our time holed up in a hotel, we just decided to come home."

Internally, Rian sighed with relief because he hated the idea that they'd come home because of his case, but he was a little apprehensive about Kane knowing there was something going on between him and CoCo. "That sucks," he said, commiserating. "Well, did you get your deposit back at least?"

"Of course," Kane said, grabbing their luggage from the back and swinging it clear of the bed to drop it to the ground as Laci got out of the truck and stretched with a groan. "But they were so nice about the situation that they offered a free stay once the situation has been fixed. We didn't have the heart to say no even though we were a little leery about staying in a place where pipes explode in the middle of the night."

"Well, it is Montana. God's country and all that."

Kane laughed and Laci rounded the truck to tuck Rian into a hug. "Hey there, brother-in-law, how are you? I heard you're working quite a case."

He lowered his voice so CoCo didn't chance to overhear. "Well, not exactly a case, as the FBI is doing the heavy lifting. I'm just looking out for a client while they finish up the investigation. We had a scary incident and I thought it best to hide out here for a few days. You don't mind, do you?"

"Of course not. What a dumb question. Where is she?" Laci asked, peering around Rian. "Is she in the house? I want to meet her. I've never met an Italian heiress before."

"And she's never met a country music star. The two of you should get along famously," Rian said, grinning as he gestured toward the house. "Yeah, she's in there finishing up a pie. And don't go teasing her about her kitchen skills. She wanted to try her hand at baking a pie this morning and I jumped in to help when it was all about to end up in the trash."

"Let me guess…dough wouldn't cooperate?"

"Yeah, not enough water."

"Classic mistake. It's happened to the best of us."

Kane rolled his eyes. "Are you two hens finished?"

Laci shot him a saucy look and said as she sashayed up the steps, "This hen will remember that comment when you're bellyaching for my famous peach pie."

Instantly contrite, Kane followed with their luggage. "Aw, baby, you know I was kidding. Don't go making threats like that." She stopped and presented her cheek, which Kane happily kissed, and she giggled. "Does this mean I'm forgiven?"

"I'll think about it."

Kane followed Laci into the house and Rian shook his head wondering when Laci had lopped off his brother's nuts and tucked them into her fancy purse, because that wasn't the brother who used to be the alpha dog. He chuckled and followed, eager to see CoCo's reaction to a real-life country music star walking into the kitchen.

COCO WAS JUST finishing up wiping down the counters when Laci McCall, a bona fide country music star, A-lister and overall mega-talented stunner, walked into the kitchen with an inquiring smile along with her husband, Kane. "You must be CoCo Abelli," she said, extending a hand as if they were just two normal people.

Kane waved with a quick introduction and then disappeared into the bedroom with the luggage, leaving Laci and CoCo alone.

"Oh, my God… I'm sorry… I'm just a bit…" CoCo took quick stock of her attire and blushed to her roots. She looked like a country bumpkin harlot in her booty shorts and tight tank. "I don't usually dress like this," she said with a slight stretch of the truth, dusting off the flour that seemed everywhere. "I didn't expect anyone to be around. Warren said he was going to some town a few miles over and…"

Laci laughed and waved away CoCo's embarrassment. "Honey, stand down. We don't put much attention on what you're wearing around the ranch. You look fine to me. And frankly, if I had that ass, I'd be wearing booty shorts like that, too. Although, I doubt any work would get done because Kane would be carrying me into the bedroom every five minutes."

The easy way Laci shared personal stuff eased CoCo's nerves enough to relax. "It's an honor to meet you. I love your music. Can I fangirl gush for a minute?" she asked, a little apologetic. "I mean, I'm sure that gets old, right?"

"Never gets old," Laci said, winking. "That's what I signed up for, you know? Please, fangirl all you want."

"Okay, just this once, I promise. Your single 'Kentucky Rain' always makes me cry, but in a good way.

It's one of those songs that just reaches into my soul and does something that I can't explain. I love that whole CD."

"'Kentucky Rain,' I love that song, too," Laci said, smiling. "I wrote that song in a day and I've found that songs that come together like that, just like pieces of a puzzle clicking together, are the ones that come from a special place. I'm glad that you were touched by my music. Makes me happy inside."

CoCo smiled, already loving Laci even though they'd just met. "You're nicer than I imagined you would be," she blurted just in time for Rian to hear.

"Yeah, well, if you want to see her temper, you ought to be her Pictionary partner. She's brutal."

"What can I say? I play to win," she said with a playful grin. "And don't let Rian fool you. He's as competitive as me, which is why we're not allowed to be partners anymore." Then she whispered conspiratorially, "We always decimate the competition."

Kane returned, sniffing the air. "Pie?"

"Oh! Um, yeah. Apple. I was bored and thought I'd give it a try. It wasn't as easy as I thought it would be. That'll teach me to use a YouTube video as my example."

"All it takes is practice, honey. I burned my first pie," Laci admitted.

Rian cracked a laugh at the memory. "Oh, yeah, that thing was toast but Kane acted like it was the best thing he'd ever eaten."

"That's love right there," CoCo said, laughing. "Did you know right then that he was the one?"

Laci shared a sparkling look of love with Kane and said, "I always knew that. Didn't need a pie to tell me that. But it sure helped my ego some."

A person would have to be blind to miss the obvious electrical current flowing between Kane and Laci. It was almost mesmerizing to see two people so connected, and the fact that their story was so romantic... CoCo couldn't help but feel misty and gooey inside. She wanted that kind of love someday.

She risked a glance at Rian and quickly dragged her focus back to the über-lovey-dovey couple and came crashing back to earth. There was no denying that she and Rian had some kind of intense physical attraction, but what would happen when they returned to Los Angeles? Their lives weren't conducive to including one another and that made her wish things were different.

Laci yawned and said, "Oh, man, I think the drive just caught up with me. Do you mind if we catch some shut-eye for a little bit and then we can talk more at dinner?"

"No, of course not," she murmured, feeling a little awkward suddenly. "I'll just get out of your hair."

"You're no trouble," Laci assured her, waving as she disappeared into the bedroom and closed the door.

Kane rubbed at his eyes. "I know I should check on the cattle but I need a few winks myself. See you in a few?" he said to Rian.

"Sure. I'll get the cattle taken care of. You rest."

And then Kane followed his wife. Rian turned to CoCo, smiling. "So? What'd you think of Laci?"

"She's amazing," she whispered, gesturing wildly for him to come outside with her. Once they were out of possible earshot she sagged into the rocking chair. "I can't believe I just met Laci McCall looking like a country hooker. I'm so embarrassed."

"Country hooker? I think you look great."

While Rian's openly appreciative glance warmed her insides, she still wished she'd been wearing her sundress instead. "You don't think she thinks less of me because of it, do you?" she fretted.

"Laci? Naw, she's the least judgmental person I know. Don't worry about it." He settled in the chair beside her. "Why are you so worked up? Frankly, I'm a little surprised. Don't you hang out with famous people all the time?"

"Not A-listers. I mean, the people I hang out with… they're the party crowd. It's not as if I'm rubbing elbows with Meryl Streep. Besides, she's a different caliber altogether."

"Laci is a great person. Just treat her like you would a friend and you'll be fine, because she's the sweetest, most openhearted woman on this planet. Unless you're playing opposite of her on game night. Then she's going to rip you a new one and gloat about it." He fake grimaced. "The woman is a terrible winner and an even worse loser. But other than that…she's golden."

CoCo laughed, feeling much better. "Must be pretty cool to call Laci McCall your sister-in-law."

"It doesn't suck," he agreed with a grin.

CoCo shared a chuckle with Rian and then heard the kitchen timer go off. She popped up from the chair and rushed to get the pie out of the oven. She was even more excited now that dessert would be the pie she made from scratch. She'd never been so excited about pie.

Rian went to feed the cattle and CoCo enjoyed a lingering stare at Rian's retreating backside. She'd never tire of that view…

Oh, girl, you're just digging yourself in deeper with each passing day.

She ignored the tiny voice and focused instead on the tantalizing scent of baked apples filling the kitchen. Rian was right; baking was relaxing when you finally got it right!

20

As luck would have it Adeline and Warren went out to dinner that night, leaving the brothers and the girls in for the night, but that was okay, since it gave them a chance to visit without censoring their language for Adeline's sake.

CoCo had become more comfortable around Laci and was now pestering Laci for intel that she could use against Rian, which he wasn't sure he should encourage, but it was worth it to watch CoCo's face light up when Laci started dishing.

"Oh! Should I share the time you got yourself in a right pickle with Merry Pritchard?" Laci teased, causing Rian to blush. Of all the stories, not that one! At his obvious discomfort CoCo nodded vigorously, egging Laci on. "Okay, well, as you might imagine, Rian was quite the little charmer in high school. He had all the girls chasing after him, wanting a piece of that Dalton pie, if you know what I mean."

"I can imagine," CoCo agreed, laughing. When Rian rolled his eyes, she said, "Aw, is someone embarrassed?"

"I probably should've mentioned that Laci is a pathological liar," he quipped. "She gets away with it because she's famous and all but don't believe a word that leaves her mouth."

Laci gasped playfully in mock outrage, looking to Kane. "Are you going to let him say things like that about me? The nerve!"

"Well, you have been known to spin a tale or two," Kane said with a glint in his eye telling that he was kidding. "But go on, because I love stories where Rian gets what's coming to him."

"Merry's dad nearly skewered me on a pitchfork!"

"What'd you do with his daughter?" CoCo asked.

"Nothing she didn't want," he said, his ears heating. "And besides, she chased me for weeks! I practically had to peel her off with a spatula!"

"Merry did have a singular attachment to Rian, which I never understood, but it was hilarious to watch," Kane said.

"Yeah, totally hilarious," Rian grumbled.

"Annnnnyway," Laci said, clearing her voice to continue her story. "Rian thought it would be a good idea to take his stalker, I mean friend, out on a date, which then turned out to be a make-out sesh in her driveway. And you can imagine how that didn't end well when Merry's dad caught them."

"What were you doing making out in her driveway?"

"It was late. I figured the old man was asleep. It seemed a calculated risk," he answered sheepishly. "Besides, if anyone was the aggressor, it was Merry! She practically ripped my shirt in half!"

"Aw, poor Rian. Attacked by desperate high school girls," CoCo said, not the least bit sorry for him, although her eyes twinkled with mischief. "I'm sure you were the victim."

"I was," he insisted, looking to Kane. "C'mon, man, back me up!"

"Sorry, no can do. No one forced you to date Merry. I told you at the time it was a bad idea and if old man Pritchard hadn't been intent on putting your liver on the end of his fork, I would've let him give you some lumps because you needed a whack on the head at that time."

"Yeah, well, thankfully, I got away but Pritchard knew we were staying at the Bradford Ranch and followed me."

Laci hooted with remembered laughter. "Oh, yes! And if fire could've shot out of his eyeballs, Rian would've been a scorch mark on the grass. But Kane and Warren came to his rescue, settled old man Pritchard down with an apology from Rian and an express promise that he wouldn't come within twenty feet of Merry ever again."

"How'd that work out?" CoCo asked, curious.

"Actually, turned out to be a blessing. She got bored with trying to get me alone when I was avoiding her like the plague and she set her sights on Chase Nolan instead. I guess they were a good fit, because they got married right out of high school. Last I heard, they have five kids and a mortgage together."

"Ah, a happily-ever-after," CoCo said, delighted.

"Yeah. I guess so. The poor bastard," Rian said and the table erupted in laughter.

A moment of easy silence passed around the table and Kane brought up the case. "So any leads?" he asked.

CoCo looked to Rian and Rian answered, "Not so

far. But I'm removed from that part of the investigation. I wonder if no news is good news?"

Laci turned to CoCo. "Are you worried about your father's safety? I would be worried sick knowing that some crazy person wanted to hurt my family."

CoCo nodded. "Yes, but I know my dad has great security and they're doing everything they can to nail this nut job. I just want it to be over so I can get back to my life." Her statement hit Rian like a punch to the gut. It shouldn't have because he knew this gig was temporary, but hearing it said aloud made it so much more clear that they were just playing around and having a good time. CoCo sensed his sudden change in demeanor even though he fought to keep his expression neutral and said, "I mean, I feel lucky to have Rian looking out for me. He's been a Godsend."

"The Dalton boys are the best to have in a crisis," Laci agreed. "I always hire Kane and Rian's company now for tours. I've had my share of crazy fans. One tried to rip my dress clean off! Another practically snatched the hair from my head. You never know what kind of crazy person might be fixating on you."

"I just want my family to be safe," she murmured, shooting Rian an inquiring look, but he ignored it and chose instead to finish his beer and then rose with his dishes.

"Your cooking reminds me of Cora, God rest her soul," Rian said, pressing a kiss on top of Laci's head in a brotherly fashion. "Great chicken."

"It was nothing," Laci said, but her smile widened under the praise. Laci loved being a domestic goddess on her off-time. She said it made her feel close to Cora even though she was gone. "How long do you think you two will be here?"

"Just a few more days, I suspect," he answered, going into the kitchen to drop off the plates. Returning, he said, "Think you can put up with us for that much longer?"

"I'll weather it," Laci said with a wink. "In the meantime, I can get to know CoCo better. We can gab like girlfriends while you guys do 'guy' things."

"Sounds like a plan," he said, but his stomach was like lead. Why was he so bothered by the fact that CoCo was openly ready to go back to her old life? What else was he thinking was going to happen? And what did he want to happen? He gestured to the outside, saying, "I'm going to feed the horses."

Normally, he would've offered to help with the dishes but he needed some air. His head was on screwy after that comment and he needed to get it together. Maybe this was a blessing. He was starting to have feelings for CoCo, which had no future, so this was a great reminder that he needed to settle that shit down before things got complicated.

How much more complicated could it get than him sleeping with a client? He wanted to groan and smack his head against a post for being an idiot.

Well, at least his secret was safe. He knew CoCo wouldn't say anything. If he could just keep it together for a few more days, Kane would never know how far things had gone and he'd just have to file this experience under the file labeled "Big Dumbass Mistakes" and move on.

Except life wasn't that easy and he should've known better.

He'd just tossed the first handful of hay into Amelia's

stall when Kane entered the barn and said, "So, how long have you two been sleeping together?"

And he knew his pooch had just been screwed.

CoCo helped Laci with the dishes in the kitchen, enjoying the opportunity to spend a little more time with the effervescent woman, but as luck would have it Laci had her own agenda.

"I know it's none of my business but I couldn't help but notice the chemistry between you and Rian. Is there something going on between you two?"

CoCo hesitated. They weren't going to tell anyone about their relationship—if you could call it that—but CoCo really could use some perspective and decided to be honest. "Rian is going to kill me but, yeah, we are *kind of* seeing each other. But it's completely complicated. And we plan to break it off as soon as we return to Los Angeles."

Laci digested the information and then said, "I know it seems like it should be easy to break things off when things started off casually but I can tell you right now the chemistry between you two is hot enough to burn. It's going to be really difficult to say goodbye. Have you thought about that?"

CoCo had not been able to think of anything else. She nodded, biting her lip, and said, "I didn't plan on having feelings for Rian. I don't know how to continue what we have once we return to our worlds. The fact is, there's no way Rian would fit in my world and I don't fit in his so it seems best to end things before it gets messy."

Laci nodded. "That would be the smart thing. But if I know anything, it's that the heart never cooperates with the brain. Let me tell you a little bit about me and Kane. My daddy thought that Kane would stand in the way of my career so he convinced Kane to turn me loose and in doing so broke my heart. Sure, I recovered, but I never forgot about him, and when we saw each other again it was as if time had never passed. Our chemistry was just as undeniable as it ever was and it was like a flame to a powder keg. There were plenty of reasons why our relationship wasn't going to work. But try telling that to our hearts. In the end, the heart wants what it wants and you just have to find a way to make it work. That is, if you want Rian."

The way Laci told the story, it was so romantic but she and Rian weren't star-crossed lovers who suddenly found themselves again. In fact, the way they hooked up certainly wasn't a story she'd relish sharing. "I wish it were that simple. The thing is, I'm a different person in Los Angeles than I am here and a part of me misses the wild and crazy life I have, but then a part of me wants to do something different."

"So be different," Laci said as if it were that easy to change.

"What if I don't know how to be different? I don't want to invite Rian into the mess that is my life and drag him down with it."

"Oh, it can't be that bad," Laci reassured her but CoCo knew better.

"The very first night we met I was having a party at my mom's Malibu beach house and one of my guests got a little too touchy-feely without my permission. Rian basically tossed him out on his ass. I'm pretty sure he saved me from being assaulted."

Laci smiled. "That sounds like Rian. He's a sucker for a woman in distress."

"Yeah, and I wasn't very grateful about it, either. I was irritated that he had crashed my party and chased off my guest. You see, I did not actually believe that there was a credible threat and I thought my dad was overreacting by hiring Rian to be my bodyguard. But then I convinced Rian to go out to a club with me and my friend dosed him with a drug and I'm still trying to wrap my brain around the fact that that's part of my life. I mean, what kind of person doses another human being for their entertainment? Before I met Rian I might never have questioned that."

"We've all made decisions that we've regretted, but if you spend so much time looking backward, you'll never be able to see the great things that are right in front of you," Laci said with a warm smile. "I really wish Cora were alive so that she could lay some of that country wisdom on you. You'll just have to settle for me. Here's the thing, life is complicated. Life is messy. But that's part of the fun. If everything in life were a straight line, we would never experience the joys and wonder of those hills and valleys. My life has had its share of sorrows but I have been blessed a million times over with happiness. I choose to focus on those good things in my life rather than the dark places that I've traveled. You have to figure out which road you want to walk."

"I know." CoCo knew that Laci was right but knowing and doing something about it were two separate things. It didn't feel as if she'd only just met Laci. Rian hadn't exaggerated that Laci was a true down-to-earth person, which made it incredibly easy to share private stuff that CoCo usually kept clutched tightly to her chest. "What if I let Rian down?" she asked. "What if I can't be the person that he wants me to be?"

Laci shook her head. "You're missing the point. Don't be who Rian wants you to be…be who *you* want to be. If Rian is meant to be in your life, he'll love whoever you are."

"That's deep," CoCo murmured, struck by how wise Laci was. "You know, for the longest time I thought that nobody expected anything of me, so why should I try if no one cared? But being here, and seeing Rian work around the ranch and meeting Warren and Adeline, and you, it's made me realize that there's a whole lot more to life than the expectations that others put on you. Rian asked me if I'm still sketching and I told him I wasn't but that wasn't entirely true. I can't stop sketching. My dad is a shoemaker but at heart he's an artist. It's just that his particular canvas happens to be made from shoe leather. I guess I inherited that itch." She paused and risked rejection by asking, "Would you be willing to look at a few of my drawings? I would love your opinion."

"I would be honored," Laci answered. "Top designers are always sending me samples so I'm used to seeing stuff before it hits the runway. I can give you an honest assessment of what I think if you'd like."

CoCo nodded, her stomach flipping with anticipation. It'd been a long time since she'd shown anyone her sketches. The fact that Laci seemed genuinely interested was a huge boost to her fragile ego. "That would be awesome. Even if the idea does scare me a little. In the past I haven't dealt well with rejection."

Laci chuckled. "Nobody likes rejection. But you come from shoe royalty. My guess is that you're far more talented than you realize. Do you have your sketches with you?"

"Actually, I have them on my phone. I have an app that allows me to sketch and I store them in the cloud."

"That's amazing. I am wowed by technology these days. I'm not exactly technologically savvy. Half the time I can't figure out my damn phone. I am in awe of anyone who has mastered the apps on their phone."

CoCo laughed, wondering how she got so lucky as to meet Laci McCall and to find her so easy to talk to. "They say you should never meet your idols because they almost never measure up. But I can tell you right now, you have exceeded my expectations. You're a wonderful person and Kane is so lucky to have you."

Laci smiled, appreciating the kind comments. "You're too sweet. If anyone is lucky, it's me. Kane is my better half and I've known it since I was fifteen years old. I count Kane among my many blessings."

CoCo blinked back tears. To have something so precious, and to know it, must be an incredible gift. She didn't know if she and Rian were meant for the long haul but she knew that there was something special between them even if she had no idea how to make it work. "I can't tell you how much I appreciate your advice. It's been a long time since I've had anyone in my life worth listening to. I've surrounded myself with too many superficial people for too long. It's a nice change to listen to someone who actually knows what they're talking about."

"I did that for a long time. I think it just comes with a certain level of fame or celebrity status or even wealth, but the good news is if you have a good foundation, those things work themselves out. Eventually you get tired of the same old scene, the same old people, doing the same old things. You might've already gotten to that point. But trust me, it won't always be this way. Once you know what you want in life, and you have the confidence to go after it, nothing will ever be the same. There's this great quote that I love sharing with people and it goes like this. 'When sleeping women awaken, they move mountains.' It's really powerful and it helped me realize that the power to make change is always inside of you. If you don't like the way that your life is, then change it. You're not locked into a track. And you have more resources than most. You can do anything you want with your life. A strong woman. I see it in you. Plus, I know Rian wouldn't be interested in somebody who was weak. That's just not who he is. So whatever you want to do with your life, just go for it."

CoCo blinked back sudden tears. It wasn't like her to bare her soul. If anyone had suggested that she'd be ready to dissolve into ridiculously happy tears in front of a woman she barely knew, she would've laughed in their face. But she'd never had somebody encourage her like this and she was quickly losing the protective layer she'd insulated herself with.

CoCo wrapped Laci into a hug, unable to contain herself. "You have no idea what it means to me to hear you say this," she explained through a sheen of tears. Even though she could've held on to Laci for another long minute, she released her with a laugh, saying, "Sorry about the impromptu PDA but I just can't explain how your advice has touched me. I don't know, maybe it's all this clean air. It's messing with my brain."

"Don't apologize, sweetie," Laci said, laughing. "Genuine hugs are the best."

"Thank you again. I really appreciate it. You've given me a lot to think about."

Laci nodded and then said, "So, break out those sketches. You've got me curious now. I want to see what the new Abelli rising star is going to be like."

CoCo blushed but eagerly went to find her phone. Laci McCall wanted to see her sketches and she'd successfully baked a pie. The day was ending on a really good note. At this rate, she could almost completely forget that some crazy person was trying to kill her.

21

RIAN SHOULD'VE KNOWN that Kane would miss nothing. It was a waste of time to lie so Rian met his brother's stare. What could he say? "Are you going to bust my balls about this? Because it's complicated."

Kane grunted in answer and pushed off the barn door, coming toward him. "I know it's about to get a hell of a lot more complicated when the father finds out that you're banging his daughter—the daughter you're supposed to be protecting."

"Ah, so you are going to bust my balls," he muttered. "Look, I know I screwed up. I don't know what to say— some things happened between us and now we can't seem to stop." His cheeks flared as if he were a boy caught with his pants down and he got flustered. Trying to explain himself just made it worse. "Mind your own business, Kane. I've got this handled."

"And how exactly do you have it *handled*? Because the chemistry you were throwing at the table was enough to catch the linens on fire."

It wasn't his fault that CoCo made his eyes cross. She was the most beautiful woman he'd ever laid eyes on. "I don't need a lecture from you. I understand the consequences."

Kane disagreed, not willing to let it go. "I don't think you do. Because I can't imagine that you would've risked everything for a piece of ass."

Rian's temper flared. "She's not a piece of ass. Don't talk about CoCo that way."

"Well, I can't imagine why you would do something so stupid. For crying out loud, Rian, you couldn't have waited until the job was over? There are plenty of fish in the sea but this one was off-limits."

"I know that!"

"Then why did you cross that line?" Kane wasn't letting him off the hook. And maybe that was a good thing but it was really pissing Rian off. "Just how do you see this ending? I don't see it ending well. What's going to happen when you move on? What if she gets jealous and starts making trouble? What if she wants to get even when you break things off and goes and tells her dad that you two were messing around? This is our company's reputation on the line."

"Why would you think that she'd do anything like that?" Rian scowled. "She's not that kind of person."

But then he thought of CoCo and his first impression of her and he paused. Was that the real CoCo and what he was seeing now was an act? He didn't want to believe that but maybe he was being a fool. "She and I already made an agreement that once we return to Los Angeles it's over. Just leave it at that. Can't you trust that I would never put our company in jeopardy?"

Kane shook his head, angry. "Before this moment I would've agreed with you but now that I know you've been sleeping with a client, I don't know what to think. You screwed up, Rian. Take responsibility."

"I am taking responsibility. I won't let anything happen to our company."

"See that it doesn't. You need to end this now. Don't wait until Los Angeles. End it today."

Rian knew Kane was right. He never should have acted on his impulse but there something about CoCo that sparked a fire so intense that it burned with delicious heat. Still, he'd known all along that they were on borrowed time. He glared at his brother. "Don't say anything to CoCo. Let me handle it," Rian said gruffly. "You're not exactly known for your tact."

"Fine. But by tomorrow, it better be done."

Kane left the barn and Rian stood there feeling like a chastised child. His dignity was trashed and his pride was definitely bruised. But there was something else, something beneath all of that, that bubbled and churned. He simply didn't *want* to end things with CoCo. That was the bald truth—the truth that he held back because he knew Kane wouldn't understand. Kane would never mess with a client. Until now, neither would Rian. But there was something about CoCo that made him want to throw every rule he'd ever held for himself into the trash. He looked to Amelia, who was slowly chewing on her hay, nickering with satisfaction. "You got any suggestions, girl? Because I think I'm screwed."

Amelia flicked her gaze away from Rian as if to say, *You're on your own, kid*, and returned to her meal. He sighed. "Yeah, that's how I feel, too. Now I have to find a way to tell CoCo that whatever we had has to stop."

Yeah, he was really looking forward to that conversation.

He walked into the farmhouse, his steps as heavy as his heart, but the minute he saw CoCo's flushed expression and the open look of delight and joy in her eyes the words died on his tongue.

She came up to him in a rush. "Oh, my God, you're not going to believe this but I showed my sketches to Laci and she absolutely loved them! She says I have talent! Can you imagine that? Me! Talented! I mean, my dad has always said that I was talented and so did my teachers but I never knew if they were just saying that because of who I was. But Laci has no reason to lie to me. And she said she would be honest. She said that she's going to show my sketches to her costume designer. If I can have a prototype made in a few months, she'll test them out on tour. I mean, there's a lot of work that has to be done before now and then but I'm just so excited because she thinks that I have what it takes to make it in this industry. And she would know, she has so much experience."

He couldn't rain on her parade. There was no way. And he liked seeing her so happy. Telling her it was over could wait until tomorrow. And since there was no sense in hiding their relationship now, he looped his arms around her and pulled her in for a tight hug. "See? I told you you have nothing to worry about. How about you let me see those sketches? I've never worn a heel but I've certainly appreciated plenty."

She giggled and sagged against him, curving her body to his in the sweetest gesture as she rose up and buried her nose against his neck, murmuring in a private voice, "Let's call it a night. I have a few things I can show you."

He groaned as her nimble fingers burrowed behind

his fly to find his cock and grab a handful of his quickly swelling flesh. A low, throaty laugh followed as he scooped her into his arms and sealed his mouth to hers.

Hell, bad news didn't have a shelf life. No sense in ruining an otherwise great day with news that could wait.

He took her to the bedroom and tossed her on the bed. She wiggled out of her clothes faster than he managed to fly out of his jeans and within seconds he was on her, kissing, touching, tasting. He couldn't get enough. He refused to listen to the little voice in his head warning him off his current decision. Hell, life was short and when a naked woman was pushing you to the bed and straddling you, you went with it.

Sure, it's just about the sex, that damn voice mocked. If that were the case, he could've easily turned CoCo down because he could get sex anywhere. It was about the feel of CoCo bearing down on his cock, the way her eyelids fluttered shut on a feminine moan as her sweet pussy swallowed his thick length and the feel of her shuddering as he hammered her G-spot with single-minded intent.

Everything about CoCo turned him on. He loved the way her Italian roots showed as she argued with him, he found her sexy and alluring…and irritating as hell when she was being stubborn, but it was the entire package that he craved.

Having CoCo in his arms was like discovering sex for the first time. "God, CoCo," he breathed, his voice a harsh rasp as she rode him hard, her beautiful breasts pearling as her hips rolled, sliding on his cock as she demanded her own pleasure.

He loved how she wasn't shy about what she wanted

and she took what she needed without apology. She was the hottest lover he'd ever had the privilege of having but even if she'd been a shy and sweet woman, he would've given his right nut to have her because it was CoCo.

His hands filled with her plump ass, guiding her as they both climbed that sexual peak together. Their breath quickened as sweat gathered on their bodies, the smell of sex and passion creating a hot musk that drove them harder. Ah, the smell of them together was an intense aphrodisiac and he wanted to flip her on her back and drive his tongue deep into her sweet core so he could taste on his tongue her unique flavor. He could spend a lifetime between her lovely thighs but he was too locked on target to stop, to even prolong the pleasure between them.

CoCo gasped, her cheeks flushed, and suddenly she stiffened, her thighs shaking as she came, and he quickly followed, spilling like a tsunami deep inside her, milked by the rhythmic contractions of her inner sheath as she fell forward with a satisfied sigh.

"Oh, Rian…you're amazing," she breathed and he swelled with manly pride. He cradled her in his arms and smoothed the damp hair from her crown. She settled more comfortably against him and murmured with a drowsy smile in her voice, "Best day ever."

He smiled even though her simple sentiment pricked his conscience. How was he going to walk away from her as Kane expected him to? CoCo was in his blood. And he liked it. How was he supposed to break things off now? He didn't have a clear answer. And the fact that CoCo felt perfectly snug in his arms didn't help.

Worrying about tomorrow's problems only ruins today.

Cora's voice sliced through his turbulent thoughts and he realized the old girl had never been wrong. He tightened his hold on CoCo and decided to enjoy the moment.

Tomorrow's problems would come soon enough.

ENZO FELT AS IF ghosts from the past were coming to stake a claim on his future. The FBI agent in charge of his investigation had come to share news of the investigation so far. "Are you familiar with a man named Barto Calvino?" the agent asked.

Barto… The memory of a small boy bloomed in his memory. "I knew him when he was a child. His father was a business associate of mine many, many years ago. Why?" Enzo asked.

"We have reason to believe Barto is involved with the threats against your family. Do you know why he might have a reason to hurt your family?"

A flash of a heated argument held many years ago appeared in his mind and that familiar weight of guilt followed but he wasn't about to share his private shame with strangers. "No," he lied, lifting his chin. "I haven't seen Barto since he was a boy."

"Did you part on bad terms with his father, Vincent?"

Flustered, Enzo shifted in his chair and called for Georgina with irritation. "Where's my coffee? My throat is parched," he said when she entered the office, her sharp heels clicking on the fine marble.

Her expression professional, her fixed smile serene, she placed his coffee before him, along with several preliminary designs submitted by some of the designers hired to oversee the off-brand sold to discount stores under another name. "Your ten o'clock has cancelled," she informed him. "Would you like me to reschedule?"

"Fine, fine," he said, motioning for her to go as he lifted his cup, wishing this conversation was over. The agent waited for Georgina to leave before launching into his questions, undeterred.

"We traced the voice mail message to an old cell phone registered to Vincent Calvino but the credit card he used was listed under Barto Calvino. It's clear he isn't a criminal mastermind but we have reason to believe he's not all that interested in covering his tracks."

"Why would he do that?" Enzo asked, confused. "Either he's the world's worst criminal or he doesn't care if he's found."

"That's exactly what we thought, too. What person wouldn't care? Unless they were living on borrowed time."

Enzo stared. "What do you mean?"

"We subpoenaed Barto's medical records on a hunch and it panned out—the man is dying. He has stage-four pancreatic cancer."

"Cancer?" Enzo repeated, feeling sick to his stomach for the boy he'd once known. Barto had been a boy of only three years old when he and Vincent had parted ways. It was before CoCo had been born. That would make Barto around thirty-seven if his math was correct. Way too young to die of cancer. He knew Vincent had died several years back and he'd wanted to attend the funeral but hadn't worked up the courage. "Where is he now?"

"We had him at a run-down apartment complex but he's gone now and worse, he's left a body behind."

Enzo felt the blood drain from his face. "A body?"

"A mercenary drifter who had a reputation for doing favors for people. My guess is that Barto hired him to scare your daughter, or worse, kill her. But either way, he's not talking now. However, that means that Barto is done waiting. We're going to need the location of your daughter. I think it's time to put her in FBI custody for her own safety."

Enzo didn't know how to handle this new information. Had his pride and ambition started this wheel in motion so many years ago? And now that Barto was twisted and vengeful, how could he not shoulder the burden of that responsibility? "Maybe if I could talk to Barto, get him to see reason," he said, knowing that the time for that conversation was likely lost. He should've done the right thing. He should've made things right before it'd come to this. His heart heavy, he said, "He was a good boy. I don't understand how things could've changed so much."

The agent, not interested in the past, shrugged. "Who's to say? Mr. Abelli, I know you hired a private protection service but they're out of their depth at this point. Barto is using whatever resources he has left for one purpose—to destroy your life, and that puts your daughter right in his sights. We'd feel more comfortable if your daughter was in custody so we can focus on finding Barto."

He sighed. The agent was right. He couldn't take chances anymore, particularly if Barto was determined to go down in a hail of gunfire.

Enzo nodded slowly, wrote down the address Rian had given him and slid it over to the agent. "She's there. Go get my daughter before Barto finds her."

The agent nodded and departed, leaving Enzo with a deeply saddened heart and a weight he could barely stand. He pulled his desk drawer open and pulled out an old, faded black-and-white picture of him in his younger days, standing with Vincent, two dashing young men with the future in their eyes and ambition in their hearts.

"*Mi dispiace*, Vincent." *I'm sorry, old friend.*

Was there any way to make amends before it was too late? He didn't know how but perhaps it was time he tried.

22

CoCo AWOKE, EAGER to start the day—a feeling she'd never actually enjoyed before—and rolled over to awaken Rian with a passionate kiss that ended with a mischievous smile. God, he was gorgeous. Those sleepy eyes and stubborn mouth were enough to send her into orbit. There must be something magical about the Bradford Ranch because since arriving she'd been nothing but happy.

"What's that for?" he asked, smiling, still half-asleep. "Not that I'm complaining."

"I can't wait to get up, get moving and start the day. Want coffee?" She started to hop out of bed but he caught her hand and pulled her back. "Oh! Rian!" she dissolved into a fit of giggles when he rubbed his stubble across her neck.

"What's the rush?" he asked, his arm wrapped around her belly and holding her close. She could get used to this. He squinted at the morning sun streaming into the bedroom and sighed as if remembering there was work waiting for him. "There are some things I don't miss about the country," he admitted.

"I figured you'd be out of bed already to feed the cattle."

"That's Kane's job. I left him to it."

She noted the subtle sour note to his voice and she called him on it. "Everything okay between you and Kane?"

He sighed and rolled away, surprising her when he climbed from the bed, fabulously naked until he jerked on a pair of jeans, concealing the view of his perfect ass. He turned back to her, all sense of drowsy softness gone from his gaze. He pushed his hand through his hair in an agitated manner before scooping up a shirt and pulling it on. "Look, we have to talk."

"That sounds ominous."

"Yeah, it's…not a great conversation."

She lost her smile. "What do you mean? What's going on? Is it something with my dad? Is he okay?"

"He's fine. I'm sorry, it's not about the case. Well, it sort of is, but it really has to do with us."

Now she was confused. They'd spent half the night exhausting each other and the rest of the night curled in each other's arms but she got the distinct impression that he was…breaking up with her. "Okay…so out with it," she told him, trying not to show that she was shaking inside.

"We both knew that this was a temporary thing and, well, it was all good as long as no one knew about it, but Kane knows and I can't risk the company's reputation by continuing to mess around with you."

"*Mess* around with me?" she repeated, stung. "Stop calling it that. I'm not a booty call."

"You know I don't feel that way," he said, with the

nerve to glower. "But we both knew that this wasn't anything we were going to publicize."

"Yeah, I know, but I thought that maybe things had changed," she said, cringing at how stupid she sounded. Of course things hadn't changed. She was just a convenient way to dip his wick. Fabulous. Her cheeks flared with embarrassed heat and she wanted to cry. So much for her wonderful morning.

"Things did change," he admitted, seeming caught between a rock and a hard place, but she was out of sympathy. "I like you a lot, CoCo, but you have to admit that our worlds just don't mesh, so what were we doing? We were playing with fire and I can't afford to let the company get burned."

"How nice of you to come to that revelation after we had sex," she said coolly. "You could've let me know last night that you'd come to this decision instead of waiting until after you'd gotten laid."

He winced. "I know it's bad timing. I was going to tell you last night but then you were so excited about your sketches and I didn't want to ruin the night."

"Thank you for leading me on," she said icily. "I feel so much better knowing that you offered me a pity romp in the sack for the sake of preserving my good mood."

"Oh, c'mon, it's not like that. You're twisting my words all up."

"No, that was pretty much exactly what you said. You're the one saying this shit. I'm just the one flabbergasted at your nerve."

"It's not as if we were dating," he reminded her. "We were just having a good time, right?"

"Sure, Rian. That's exactly what we were doing." But tears sprang to her eyes and she hated that she felt so broken at the idea of breaking up that she couldn't stay another minute in that room with him for fear of embarrassing herself further by openly bawling. "Thanks for the memories," she said and then bolted.

Rian was smart enough to stay behind.

KANE SAW COCO run down the stairs and exit through the front door, tears streaking her face, and he knew Rian must've delivered the news. He set his coffee cup down and caught Laci's confused stare but before he could explain, Rian bounded down the stairs to glare at him as he said, "It's done. Happy?" and then chased after CoCo, though in his opinion he should've let the girl walk off some steam. He returned to his coffee but Laci had put two and two together.

"What'd you do?" she asked, annoyed. "I have a feeling your hands are all over this one. Fess up. What'd you make that boy do?"

"He's not a boy, he's a man, and if he'd thought like a man, he wouldn't have put himself in this position."

"Answer me." Laci propped her hands on her hips. "Please tell me you did not meddle in their relationship."

"That's exactly the problem. There shouldn't have been a relationship. She's a client. We have a hands-off policy and you know it. Without it, where's the integrity? Trust me, it's better this way. Less mess."

"Sometimes life's messy," she said, slapping her oven mitt down. "And you of all people should know that. And while I understand that you have to do things to protect your reputation, if you can't see that your brother is in love with that woman, you're blind as a bat."

He scoffed. "In love? Not hardly. I know you're a

romantic at heart and you like to play matchmaker but Rian's a player, not a guy comfortable with a commitment. I'm doing that poor girl a favor."

"Kane Dalton, that's not your job to judge. Shame on you for being a meddling fool in business that's none of your concern. You're right, Rian is an adult, so you better let him make his own choices instead of bullying him into making choices that *you* think are right for him. He loves her. And you just made him break up with her. Sort of like when my daddy made you break up with me. How'd that make you feel?"

Damn the woman had a sharp tongue but a sharper mind. Was he making the same mistake? But Rian had known better! "Rian knew not to mess with a client," he said stubbornly. "This is on him, not me."

"Has Rian ever broken that rule before?" she asked, crossing her arms and glaring.

"No," he had to admit.

"Then what makes you think he would lightly trip over something so big? He didn't mean to fall in love, you big dolt. No one does. That's the beauty of it. I spent a good portion of my time last night after dinner convincing that poor girl to take a chance and then you sent Rian to crush her heart, making me out to be a liar!"

Aw, hell. How was he supposed to know what the women were laughing and carrying on about in the kitchen after dinner? The tips of his ears burned but his stubborn tongue refused to admit he'd stepped over the line. Not that he had to. Laci was burning a hole in his head with that blazing fury directed straight at him. "This is just the way it has to be—"

"Bullshit. Don't you go selling me a bag of goods

when you know full well you screwed up and put your nose where it didn't belong. I can't believe you, Kane. Your brother is a good man and you need to trust that he can handle himself. And for the record, I like her. I like her a lot. She's spunky and courageous and she isn't put off by that Dalton obstinate streak that'll likely be the death of you both!"

Laci scooped up her oven mitt and marched back to the kitchen, leaving him slack-jawed at the verbal ass-chewing she'd just given him. *How am I the bad guy in this?* He thought of Rian and how up to this point he'd never so much as crossed a toe over the line in spite of being a consummate player, always keeping things professional in spite of the aggressive women that sometimes waved their tails beneath his nose, and he realized he might've overreacted to the situation.

He took the last swallow of coffee in his mug and prepared to make amends, if only to get back in the good graces of his wife, but as he walked to the screen door and stepped out on the porch everything seemed to move in slow motion as shots rang out and CoCo, emerging from the barn, crumpled to the ground, and Rian dived to cover her fallen body with his own.

"Stay back!" he said to Laci when she came running. "Go to the bedroom and lock the door!"

Laci didn't waste time arguing and fled up the stairs. He reached into the armoire by the door and pulled his gun. Who the hell was out there? And how did they find the ranch?

"WHAT THE HELL have you done?" Rian screamed, holding pressure against CoCo's stomach where a fountain of blood was spilling onto the dust. He looked at the stranger walking toward him, the man's gun pointed straight at him, but he didn't care about dying. He'd let CoCo down. He'd brought her all the way to Kentucky and she'd been shot anyway!

Tears blinded him but he had to keep pressure on the wound. "Who are you? Why have you done this? What'd she ever do to you?" He was babbling, losing his cool and his training, but he'd never held the woman of his dreams dying in his arms before and he lost all sense of objectivity. He was at a disadvantage. He could only hope that Kane could get to him before the man blew his head off, too.

"The entire Abelli line deserves to die for being the thieving liars they all are," the man said with a thick Italian accent. "Her father stole my father's work and passed it off as his own. Then pushed my father out of the company without so much as a penny for his vision. We lived in poverty while Enzo's star rose. Enzo Abelli is a thief and a crook. His blood will run with his daughter's but first, he must know loss." He cocked the gun and leveled it at Rian with a dispassionate stare. "Goodbye, Mr. Dalton."

A second shot rang out but when Rian expected to feel the rip of a bullet tearing through his flesh, the Italian dropped to the ground in a heap. Rian whipped his gaze around, shocked to see Warren with his smoking shotgun.

"Son of a bitch comes onto my land and starts shooting up the people I love? Not happening on my watch! Adeline, call 911, the girl's been hit."

Rian sagged with relief at not being dead but the feeling was short-lived as CoCo was still leaking like a sieve and growing paler by the minute. Good God, she was going to die in his arms. He saw Kane run out and do a quick perimeter search to make sure the Italian had been working alone.

Kane jogged over to Rian, concern in his eyes. "She's going to make it, buddy," he promised, though his eyes told another story.

Tears blinded Rian as he tried to keep CoCo from bleeding out, but there was so much blood. A gut shot... It was usually a game ender. "I don't know where he came from. He just popped out of his car and shot her. I wasn't paying attention. It's my fault. It's my fault!"

"Stop it!" Kane said sternly, getting his attention. "We don't have details and in the absence of details we deal in facts. What we know is that he's dead and he's not going to hurt anyone else. Now we have to focus on CoCo."

Rian jerked a nod and swallowed, getting a hold of himself. The sound of ambulance sirens splitting the air sent a wave of shaky relief through him. Kane waved the ambulance over and it stopped short of Rian and CoCo in a puff of dust as the sheriff deputies rolled in behind the ambulance. It was a three-ring circus but Rian only cared about CoCo.

Why'd he let her go off by herself into the barn? Why'd he go and do something as stupid as saying he wanted to end things? If he'd just kept his mouth shut, they would've been in the bedroom still, and maybe they would've seen the strange Italian pull up and they could've stopped him. Too many questions without answers. He climbed into the ambulance with CoCo, refusing to leave her. He didn't care who the man was at the moment. He just wanted to make sure CoCo was going to be okay. They'd find the answers to every-thing else later.

Fight, baby. Fight.

23

CoCo HAD NEVER truly believed in miracles until she'd somehow woken in a hospital, bandaged and alive after a twelve-hour surgery to put her guts back together. She wasn't dead and that in itself, according to her doctor, was a damn miracle.

Being shot in the stomach was pretty much going to kill most people, unless the bullet somehow, by the grace of God, missed every vital organ and only nicked her liver on its way out. Yeah, talk about miracles.

Pain bloomed in her body as she tried shifting in bed, nearly blacking out from the intensity of the agony. Okay, so surviving a gut shot wasn't all ice cream and rainbows. The pain would be enough to make her scream if it weren't for that lovely morphine drip that came whenever she pushed a button. Today was the first day she'd felt up to talking to anyone and everyone wanted a little time at her bedside.

She had so many questions but she wasn't sure if she was up to the answers. Even though she'd been losing consciousness, she'd heard what that man had said. Her father? A crook? What did that mean?

Rian walked in and a weak smile found her lips. Her heart lightened at the sight of him even though it shouldn't. But he'd thrown himself over her body and that meant something. She just didn't know what it meant in the big scheme of things. Would he do that for any client? Or was he prepared to die with her?

"How are you feeling?" he asked, going to sit beside her, taking her hand into his. "Your color is better. You had us going for a while."

"I like to keep people on their toes," she said with a weak smile.

"You definitely did that." His gaze roved her face and her heart nearly broke at the raw emotion she saw there. That was no act. Whatever he was feeling, it was real and she was relieved. "Your dad is anxious to see you. Are you feeling up to talking to him?"

"Who was that man?" she asked, confused. "I'd never seen him before in my life. He seemed so normal when he stepped out of the car. I thought he was a friend of Warren's or something. But then he…took out a gun and just sh-sh-shot me. No hesitation whatsoever."

As difficult as it was for her to get the words out, it seemed equally so for Rian to relive that moment. "His name was Barto Calvino and he was the son of a man who worked with your father before you were born. He was sick, and he knew he wasn't going to make it much longer. So when he pulled the trigger, he had nothing to lose."

"Why would he hate my father so much?" she asked, pained. "My father is the sweetest man on the planet."

"I think that's something you and your dad should talk about," he said gently. "I'm going to let you get a

few minutes with him. He's been here since you went
into surgery."

She nodded, blinking back tears. She wanted to ask
Rian to stay but after everything that had happened, she
didn't know where they stood. The last words between
them were Rian breaking up with her. She didn't want
him to stay with her out of pity. She wanted him to stay
because he wanted to be with her, even if they didn't
know how their worlds would mesh. She wanted him
to not care about that stuff, to care only about her. Rian
let himself out and her father, looking older than ever
before, walked in, a wealth of worry and relief etched
in his expression.

He took her hand and kissed it, patting it lovingly
even as his eyes watered.

"Babbo," she said, her eyes watering, as well. "I'm
okay. Please don't cry."

"I'm so sorry for putting you in this position. It's
all my fault."

She shook her head. "Don't blame yourself, please."

He shook his head resolutely before sitting heavily
in the seat beside her bed. "No, I have something to tell
you. It's something I'm not proud of but it's time you
know my secret shame."

CoCo frowned, scared of what possible secrets her father had been keeping, but she had to be mature enough
to handle the information. Whatever it was, they'd handle it together. "Go ahead, *Babbo…* I'm listening."

"Vincent and I were best friends. We shared a dream
of creating fine shoes for upstanding gentleman. Vincent was the quiet one while I was the one who wasn't
afraid to talk. One day he sketched a design… It was
brilliant. Even to my amateur eye, I knew it was some-

thing special. But I told him the opposite. I manipulated him into thinking it was trash. He discarded the idea, trusting me." His voice wavered. "But I knew I had to get him out of the company or else it might happen again. We fought. I started a rumor that he had stolen from the company. Back then your honor and dignity were worth more than gold. You could get a loan simply based on your integrity. I made it so that no one would ever believe him if he tried to say that I had taken his idea. I sold my soul to the devil for the riches we have today and you nearly paid with your life for my greedy ambition. Can you forgive me?"

CoCo was stunned. There was no better word for it. Her silence caused her father to cry.

"You hate me, I understand. I am nothing. Vincent was the talent and I stole it. Barto wanted to make me pay for killing his father's spirit. I deserve it. He should've aimed that bullet at me."

"Stop, *Babbo*," she said gently, hating that her father carried such guilt over something he'd done so many years ago. "What you did was wrong, but if Vincent was truly that talented, he would've been able to create new visions, new sketches. You are talented, too. You were ambitious. You had what it took to get ahead and create a name for yourself."

"Don't let me off the hook, sweetheart. I need to make amends."

"Barto is dead. It doesn't matter his reasons, what he did was worse than what you did. He took the coward's way out."

He nodded. "But I can't blame him for his rage. He was trying to avenge his father."

"This isn't fifteenth-century Italy. You can't go around

shooting people because they screwed you out of a good idea," she replied, her head beginning to throb. She closed her eyes briefly, needing a minute, then reopened them. "*Babbo*, it's over. Let's start fresh."

"How?"

CoCo licked her lips, suddenly parched, and her father quickly handed her a cup of water. She took several swallows before gaining the courage to admit that she'd been sketching. "I want to join the family business. But," she cut in when he started to babble happily, "I'm not designing men's shoes. I want to design women's shoes. I have a few designs I want to show you if you're willing to bend a little in what you think the Abelli brand is all about."

She expected a gentle but surefire *no* because that's what her father had always done when she'd approached him about designing heels but this time he simply nodded. Maybe her brush with death had made him realize that he'd been hanging on to all the wrong things but CoCo wasn't about to look a gift horse in the mouth.

"I would be honored to start over with you, my daughter. I've been stubbornly clinging to my own ways for too long. Perhaps it's time for a woman's touch."

CoCo smiled, exhausted but happy. "Thank you, *Babbo*. I'm going to work hard not to disappoint you."

Enzo ran a knuckle lightly across her cheek, his gaze filled with love. "You could never. It is I who will work to not disappoint you with my stubbornness."

She would've laughed but she feared the pain and simply smiled. "I've recently had some experience with a stubborn man. I think I can handle you."

He laughed but didn't ask who she was referring to and she was grateful. She wasn't sure what was happening between her and Rian and at the moment, she was too tired to figure it out.

THE CASE WAS OVER. There was really no reason to hang around anymore. CoCo's father was here, the FBI were coordinating with the local sheriff to deal with the body of Barto Calvino and since Rian wasn't in charge of the investigation, his part was finished.

But he couldn't leave CoCo. Laci and Kane showed up in the waiting room and Laci folded him into a hug. "So what's the word?" she asked, concerned.

"I don't know, her dad was in there with her. I wanted to give them some privacy," he said, feeling lost and useless. He looked to Kane. "I'll get the report filed—"

"Screw that. Don't worry about the paperwork. Look, I'm so sorry about how this all went down," Kane admitted, looking to Laci for reinforcements. She gave him an imperceptible nod and he continued, "I overstepped when I insisted that you break things off with CoCo. I should've realized that you'd never put the company in danger. The fact that you were willing to die for her tells me that she's something special and I was too blind to see it. I'm sorry, man, for being such a dick." Laci nudged him with her elbow. "And I'm glad your girl didn't die."

The old Rian would've balked at the implication that he'd fallen head over heels for a woman but he didn't feel the least bit reluctant to admit it out loud. The reason he couldn't bring himself to leave was because CoCo had ceased being just another client. Their fates had been sealed from day one even if neither had realized it. "I do love her," he said simply, feeling a whoosh of relief wash over him. "I can't explain it. But I love her and I'm not leaving this hospital until she leaves with me."

Laci squealed and clapped her hands together. "Oh, Rian! I'm so happy for you! And I'm so happy for CoCo, too! Now, go in there and tell her how you feel. Quick! Before you lose your nerve and something gets in the way."

Rian hesitated. Her dad was still in there. He didn't want to interrupt. But as he started walking, he passed Enzo leaving CoCo's room and the two paused before Rian thrust his hand out, his voice threatening to betray his nervousness. "Sir, I love your daughter. I didn't mean to fall in love with her but I did and I understand if you don't appreciate my feelings but I'm not going anywhere until she leaves this hospital with me. I hope you can understand that. I also hope that maybe someday you can forgive me for falling in love while on the job because it's going to be awfully awkward around the dinner table during holidays if we're not able to get along. Not to mention, I want our kids to know their grandfather."

"Kids?" The older man's bushy eyebrows rose as he stared, openly assessing him. "Is that so?"

He swallowed. "Not yet, sir, but eventually."

Enzo, a formidable man in his own right, paused and then said, "Marry her first and we'll talk. Until then... be a gentleman and keep your hands to yourself."

Rian would've promised the moon. All he heard was Enzo had given them his blessing...even if it came with a stern condition. "Yes, sir," he said, bobbing his head. "Won't touch her until the wedding."

Enzo chuckled and walked away. It was then that

Rian realized he might've just made a promise he wouldn't be able to keep.

He returned to CoCo's room and immediately kissed her. Her eyelids fluttered open and she smiled, a little unsure and he didn't blame her.

"What are you doing? You don't have to stay any longer," she said quietly, searching his gaze. "I appreciate everything you've done for me—"

"Marry me," he blurted out and she stopped, shocked. "What?"

"Um, yeah, marry me," he said with a resolute nod. There was no turning back now. He knew what he wanted and didn't care if anyone else thought he was being impetuous, spontaneous or just plain nuts. He knew how he felt about CoCo and it wasn't likely to change, so why waste time? "I just promised your dad that I wouldn't touch you again until after the wedding so…yeah, that might've been a tall order. How do you feel about a quickie courthouse wedding?"

She stared at him. Was she overwhelmed or wondering if he was crazy for thinking that she might want to marry him? And then she broke out into smiles and tears and pulled him weakly to her so she could kiss him again. He was careful not to hurt her but he was so relieved that she hadn't told him to pound sand. He pulled away, searching her gaze. "So…is that a yes?"

"To the worst proposal ever?" she asked.

He nodded sheepishly because he had to admit that hadn't been the way he'd imagined asking the woman of his dreams to be his forever but hey, as long as she said yes, he didn't care.

"Yeah, pretty much," he said and she grinned more

broadly, which he took as a good sign. "So courthouse quickie as soon as you're able?"

"Oh, I'll marry you, but hell no to the courthouse quickie. I'm Italian. You're crazy if you think my family can fit in a courthouse. No, my wedding will be in Italy at my father's villa and it will be the biggest, most off-the-charts sensation that you've ever seen. So prepare yourself. My Italian cousins are a handful."

He didn't care. He'd agree to anything. Except... "Do you think your dad was serious about not touching until the wedding?"

She nodded. "Like a heart attack." But as Rian groaned, wondering how he was going to manage to keep that promise, she whispered, "But what he doesn't know won't hurt him. My father likes to think I've been saving myself for marriage."

Rian guffawed at that idea until he realized he'd laughed a little too loudly and CoCo scowled at the implication. He immediately sobered and said, "Whatever you want, babe. I'd do anything for you. Even if it means keeping my hands to myself while you plan the wedding of the century. Just promise me one thing..."

"Yeah?"

He got serious and cupped her hand gently. "Promise me you'll never put yourself in the path of a bullet ever again. If I live to be a hundred, I'll never get that image of you crumpling to the ground out of my head."

Her eyes watered and she nodded, then whispered, "I promise."

And that's all he needed.

Well, that and CoCo by his side for the rest of their lives.

He'd fallen hard for the Italian heiress—not bad for a country boy from Kentucky.

Both Dalton boys had done good. Damn good. Bet no one saw that one coming!

Epilogue

"No turning back now," his brother said, helping him adjust his tie because his own hands were shaking so hard. "You look great, little brother."

Rian looked to Kane and gripped his arm gratefully. "Thanks for everything. You're the reason I turned into anyone halfway decent. You made sure I was fed, safe, even got me my first job."

Kane's eyes watered but he covered with a gruff "Don't be going all mushy on me now." But then he added, "You didn't need me to be who you were meant to be. You were always a good kid and you're an even better man."

The wedding march started and he knew this was the moment he'd always been waiting for, even if he'd never known it. The woman of his dreams was going to marry him today. He could hardly believe it. A lot had happened in the year since Barto Calvino had taken his shot at CoCo and it was dizzying to try to put it all in a timeline but the highlights were simple and profound.

CoCo was now a full-fledged partner in the Abelli shoe empire, making waves with her beautiful, feminine heels that everyone seemed to want to have—helped in no small part by Laci wearing Abelli heels exclusively on her newest tour—and CoCo had realized that she'd been hiding behind a party lifestyle to keep from admitting that she was afraid of failing. Now it was hard to remember when CoCo had been a hard-core party animal because today, she was a businesswoman and artist. Except behind closed doors, then she returned to her wild roots and did things that made Rian worship at her feet.

Enzo, determined to make things right as best he could, named the newest line the *Calvino* and donated every cent of the sales to a scholarship fund in Vincent's name for aspiring designers with Italian ancestry and humble beginnings. It'd made Enzo feel good to associate something positive with Vincent instead of the unfortunate stain his son had caused, all because of something Enzo had done when he'd been young and too ambitious to see beyond his actions.

"You ready to do this?" Kane asked.

Rian met his brother's inquisitive look with a resolute one of his own. "I'm more than ready, brother. Let's do this."

"All right, then. Let's go."

Today was the start of the rest of his life, and Rian, for one, couldn't wait to get things rolling.

He and CoCo had a lifetime of lovin', fightin' and baby-makin' to do and he didn't want to waste another minute.

* * * * *

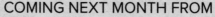

COMING NEXT MONTH FROM

HARLEQUIN®

Blaze®

Available August 18, 2015

#859 A SEAL'S TEMPTATION
Uniformly Hot!
by Tawny Weber

Lark Sommers is too busy guarding her independence to admit she needs love. Navy SEAL Shane O'Brian is too busy protecting others to realize he yearns for a woman's touch. But the passion between them is about to ignite!

#860 ONE BREATHLESS NIGHT
Three Wicked Nights
by Jo Leigh

On New Year's Eve Rick Sinclair looks like danger and sex wrapped in a tux. Already engaged teacher Jenna Delaney is about to find out if he can teach *her* a few things.

#861 THIS KISS
Made in Montana
by Debbi Rawlins

Ethan Styles is the hottest bull rider on the circuit, but he doesn't stand a chance against one very sexy bounty hunter determined to give him the ride of his life!

#862 INSATIABLE
Unrated!
by Leslie Kelly

A favor from a handsome stranger turns into an insatiable affair that Viv Callahan doesn't want to end. Until she discovers that Damian Black is a tycoon...and that's not his only secret.

YOU CAN FIND MORE INFORMATION ON UPCOMING HARLEQUIN® TITLES, FREE EXCERPTS AND MORE AT WWW.HARLEQUIN.COM.

HBCNM0815

REQUEST YOUR FREE BOOKS!
2 FREE NOVELS PLUS 2 FREE GIFTS!

(H) HARLEQUIN®

Blaze®

red-hot reads!

YES! Please send me 2 FREE Harlequin® Blaze® novels and my 2 FREE gifts (gifts are worth about $10). After receiving them, if I don't wish to receive any more books, I can return the shipping statement marked "cancel." If I don't cancel, I will receive 4 brand-new novels every month and be billed just $4.74 per book in the U.S. or $5.21 per book in Canada. That's a savings of at least 14% off the cover price. It's quite a bargain. Shipping and handling is just 50¢ per book in the U.S. and 75¢ per book in Canada.* I understand that accepting the 2 free books and gifts places me under no obligation to buy anything. I can always return a shipment and cancel at any time. Even if I never buy another book, the two free books and gifts are mine to keep forever.

150/350 HDN GH2D

Name	(PLEASE PRINT)

Address	Apt. #

City	State/Prov.	Zip/Postal Code

Signature (if under 18, a parent or guardian must sign)

Mail to the **Reader Service:**
IN U.S.A.: P.O. Box 1867, Buffalo, NY 14240-1867
IN CANADA: P.O. Box 609, Fort Erie, Ontario L2A 5X3

Want to try two free books from another line?
Call 1-800-873-8635 or visit www.ReaderService.com.

* Terms and prices subject to change without notice. Prices do not include applicable taxes. Sales tax applicable in N.Y. Canadian residents will be charged applicable taxes. Offer not valid in Quebec. This offer is limited to one order per household. Not valid for current subscribers to Harlequin Blaze books. All orders subject to credit approval. Credit or debit balances in a customer's account(s) may be offset by any other outstanding balance owed by or to the customer. Please allow 4 to 6 weeks for delivery. Offer available while quantities last.

Your Privacy—The Reader Service is committed to protecting your privacy. Our Privacy Policy is available online at www.ReaderService.com or upon request from the Reader Service.

We make a portion of our mailing list available to reputable third parties that offer products we believe may interest you. If you prefer that we not exchange your name with third parties, or if you wish to clarify or modify your communication preferences, please visit us at www.ReaderService.com/consumerschoice or write to us at Reader Service Preference Service, P.O. Box 9062, Buffalo, NY 14240-9062. Include your complete name and address.

HBI5

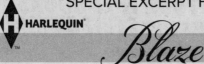
"I can do almost anything with clay. Pottery is my passion, but I really enjoy sculpting, too. Hang on." Lark smiled and held up one finger, as if Shane would leave the minute she turned around.

She swept into the storage room and bent low to get something from the bottom shelf. And Shane knew it'd take an explosion to get him to move.

Because that was one sweet view.

He watched the way the fabric of her dress sort of floated over what looked to be a Grade A ass, then had to shove his hands into his pockets to hide his reaction.

As Lark came back with something in her hand, she gave him a smile that carried a hint of embarrassment, but unless she could read his mind, he didn't know what she had to be embarrassed about.

"You might like this," she said quietly, wetting her lips before holding out her hand, palm up.

On it was a small, whimsical dragon. Wings unfurled, it looked as if it was smiling.

HBEXP0815

"You made this?" Awed at the way the colors bled from red to gold to purple, he rubbed one finger over the tiny, detailed scales of the dragon's back. "It's great."

"He's a guardian dragon," Lark said, touching her finger to the cool ceramic, close enough that all he'd have to do was shift his hand to touch her. "You might like one of your own. I can tell Sara worries about you."

Shane grimaced at the idea of his baby sister telling people—especially sexy female people with eyes like midnight—that he needed protecting. Better to change the subject than comment on that.

"It takes a lot of talent to make something this intricate," he said, waiting until her gaze met his to slide his hand over hers. He felt her fingers tremble even as he saw that spark heat. Her lips looked so soft as she puffed out a soft breath before tugging that full bottom cushion between her teeth. He wanted to do that for her, just nibble there for a little while.

"I'm good with my hands," she finally said, her words so low they were almost a whisper.

How good? he wanted to ask, just before he dared her to prove it.

Don't miss
A SEAL'S TEMPTATION by Tawny Weber.
Available in September 2015 wherever
Harlequin® Blaze® books and ebooks are sold.

www.Harlequin.com

Love the Harlequin book you just read?

Your opinion matters.

Review this book on your favorite
book site, review site, blog or your own
social media properties and share
your opinion with other readers!

HARLEQUIN®

A *Romance* FOR EVERY MOOD™

JUST CAN'T GET ENOUGH?

Join our social communities
and talk to us online.

You will have access to the latest
news on upcoming titles and special
promotions, but most importantly,
you can talk to other fans about your
favorite Harlequin reads.

Harlequin.com/Community

Facebook.com/HarlequinBooks

Twitter.com/HarlequinBooks

Pinterest.com/HarlequinBooks

THE WORLD IS BETTER WITH

Romance

Harlequin has everything from contemporary, passionate and heartwarming to suspenseful and inspirational stories.

**Whatever your mood,
we have a romance just for you!**

Connect with us to find your next great read, special offers and more.

f /HarlequinBooks

🐦 @HarlequinBooks

www.HarlequinBlog.com

www.Harlequin.com/Newsletters

⬧ HARLEQUIN®

A *Romance* FOR EVERY MOOD™

www.Harlequin.com

SERIESHALOAD2015